Read
D.W. M

An Earlier Heaven

"Marchwell has done yet another fantastic job with creating a story designed to draw the reader in and keep you compelled until the final sentence."

—Literary Nymphs Reviews

"*An Earlier Heaven* is a beautiful reminder to count your blessings no matter how big or small, and it will linger in your heart and mind long after the last page is turned."

—Long and Short Reviews

Sins of the Father

"Mr. Marchwell has created a fascinating story about three men in a contemporary setting… Thanks go to Mr. Marchwell for an inspiring story."

—Fallen Angel Reviews

"I really enjoyed this book even though it did cause me to shed a few tears. It is very well written."

—The Romance Studio

"It's a compelling story, and not the usual gay romance… It's complicated and Marchwell weaves the story well, making it quite the page turner."

—Jeff and Will

By D.W. MARCHWELL

All That Heaven Will Allow
Comfort
Falling • When Memory Fails
A Fine Mingling
Mitchell's Presence
Pictures on Silence
Sins of the Father
A Still, Small Voice
Until
Wishing on a Blue Star (Dreamspinner Anthology)

GOOD TO KNOW SERIES
Good to Know
An Earlier Heaven
Roots and Wings

Published by DREAMSPINNER PRESS
http://www.dreamspinnerpress.com

All That HEAVEN Will Allow

D.W. MARCHWELL

Dreamspinner Press

Published by
DREAMSPINNER PRESS

5032 Capital Circle SW, Suite 2, PMB# 279, Tallahassee, FL 32305-7886 USA
http://www.dreamspinnerpress.com/

All That Heaven Will Allow
© 2014 D.W. Marchwell.

Cover Art
© 2014 Bree Archer.
http://www.breearcher.com
Cover content is for illustrative purposes only and any person depicted on the cover is a model.

ISBN: 978-1-63216-166-6
Digital ISBN: 978-1-63216-167-3
Library of Congress Control Number: 2014947599
First Edition November 2014

Printed in the United States of America
∞
This paper meets the requirements of
ANSI/NISO Z39.48-1992 (Permanence of Paper).

For Lee,
I will always be grateful.

Chapter 1

"C'MON, JIMMY, how many times I gotta beg?"

The drunken fool was breathing enough whiskey into his face to pickle his liver, but Jimmy Campbell smiled anyway and looked into Billy's eyes. "Billy," he cooed softly. "Now, you know that you've got yourself a perfectly fine man at home. Maybe you quit coming in here every night hitting on me, and he might just show you how much he still loves you." *Hopefully*, Jimmy thought as he felt Billy release the death grip he had on his ass. "Now, you go on and wait outside. I'll call you a cab as usual." Jimmy turned to Ken, the new bartender, and drew his hand across his throat. Ken nodded that he understood; Billy is cut off. "Kenny, get Billy here a big mug of coffee, would you?"

"Sure thing, Boss," Ken said, smiling and nodding.

"You drink that coffee and get yourself home so you can be with your man, Billy." Jimmy started to move away, but Billy caught him by the wrist.

"He don't love me no more," Billy said, plopping himself back down at the bar. "Keeps telling me that I've been ignoring him for too long, that I'm a drunken old fool."

"That's 'cause you are, Billy." Jimmy patted him on the shoulder and then felt a little guilty. "But I tell you what I'll do for you. You don't come in here for the rest of this week, you stay sober long enough to prove that man of yours wrong about what he thinks you feel for him, and I'll treat the two of you to no cover charge for the new band we got coming in on Saturday night."

"How the hell I do that when he's never home."

Jimmy leaned in close and put his lips near Billy's ear. "You gotta give him a reason to stay home, Billy." He leaned back a little and offered Billy a sincere smile. "Fix him his favorite dinner or take him out for a nice steak. Hell, take him out and flirt with him like you been flirting with me, and I'm sure he'll come around."

"How come you got no man, Jimmy? A sweet thing like you? There's plenty of men come in here thinking you're just the sweetest thing they ever saw."

"That's why," Jimmy said as he pointed to Billy's reflection in the mirror behind the bar.

"What?" Billy furrowed his brow. "You mean the bar? You got no man because you spend all your time at the bar?"

"Yeah, sure," Jimmy said as he watched Ken laugh and turn away. "The bar's the reason." He took his cell phone and dialed the cab company, having memorized the number many, many years ago. He pushed the mug of coffee toward Billy as he listened to the rings. "Come on, now, Billy. Drink up, 'cause I'm calling your cab right now. And don't forget our deal, okay? I don't see you in here the rest of the week, you treat your man right, and you two get yourselves front-row seats Saturday night." Jimmy turned away from Billy when he finally heard a voice on the other end.

"A whole fuckin' week?" Billy sipped at his coffee.

"Today's Thursday, Billy." Ken topped up the mug and looked at Jimmy, smirking and shaking his head. "Think you can stay away for two days?"

"Two days? Fuck yeah. Be sleeping until Saturday morning," Billy said, howling with laughter as he slapped Ken on the arm. "Hey, how come you don't go after Jimmy, there? You two'd make a fine, fine couple."

"That's exactly what I told my wife, but she got upset for some reason."

"I hear that," Billy said as he took another mouthful of coffee. "Wives, huh? Can't live with 'em.... End of sentence." Billy pushed himself away from the bar. "How long you been with your man?"

"Ten years," Ken said, taking the mug and then wiping the counter with the rag that seemed to be a permanent part of his shoulder. "And done told you plenty of times, Billy. I'm married to a woman."

"Twenty-seven," Billy said, some pride evident in his voice. "Johnny and me been together for twenty-seven years."

"Congratulations," Jimmy said, closing his phone and stuffing it into his back pocket. "If you want it to be twenty-eight, you listen to me now." Jimmy started guiding Billy to the front door, careful to avoid letting Billy get too close to the other dozen patrons. "I don't want to see you in here until Saturday. And I don't want to see you already wasted. Understood?"

"What's his man's name?" Billy said, looking back over at Ken.

Jimmy wanted to slap the loveable drunk and tell him to focus. He sighed and took for granted that Billy probably wouldn't remember any of this.

"He seems like a nice guy. And the way he looks at you, I think Ken might be kind of sweet on you, Jimmy."

"I'm old enough to be his father."

"So." Billy shrugged. "That kind of shit don't matter no more. C'mon, Jimmy, quit being such an old fuddy-duddy. Now, you get over there and you ask him out, or he's gonna get away on you."

"He's already married, Billy, to a woman."

"Oh, shoot, that's right." Billy scratched his head and moved through the front door. "What'd you say his man's name is?"

"Mindy," Jimmy said as he patted Billy on the shoulder. Luckily, the cab pulled up right on time, and before Jimmy could even give the cab driver directions, Billy was passed out in the back. Jimmy recited the address and handed two twenties to the driver.

He shook his head as he headed back into the bar and wondered if he would see Billy the next day. Or would the loveable old fart be able to pull it together long enough to see a free concert? Jimmy still hadn't returned the message he'd had from that guy whose band would be there on Saturday. He pulled out his phone and searched the numbers, trying to remember if it had been a local number or not.

"You paid for his taxi again, didn't you?"

Jimmy heard Ken's question, but didn't look up; he just kept on walking and then pointed to a random section of the counter top. "You missed a spot."

"Very funny," Ken said, his OCD forcing him to pull the towel off his shoulder and swipe it over the immaculate surface a couple more times. "You did, didn't you?"

"Yes, Kenneth. I paid for his cab again."

"You're too nice to people, Boss."

Jimmy gave up trying to find the phone number and moved behind the bar. "Ken, you above all people should realize that that's a blessing and that you should quit criticizing me about it."

"I work for what I get, Jimmy." Ken took the cloth off his shoulder and moved to the opposite end of the bar, clearly upset by what Jimmy had said. "You know I appreciate what you did for me—helping me out when no one else would hire me—but I've never taken anything from you that I didn't earn."

Jimmy closed his eyes and scrubbed at his forehead. He walked back and stood beside Ken as he cleaned glasses. "I'm sorry, Kenny. You know I didn't mean it that way. And I should be the appreciative one, what with all you do around here. And I never have to ask you to do any of it. You just do it 'cause it needs doing." Jimmy reached for the apron tie at the small of Ken's back and undid the knot. "Okay. I'm sorry. I fucked up. So, I'm giving you some time off. Go home. Be with that gorgeous wife of yours. I don't wanna see you in here until Monday. Unless you think Mindy might like to hear the band on Saturday night. Then, by all means, come on back, and it'll be my treat."

Ken's eyes shifted to the door at the creaking sound it made when it opened. "I'll be right with you, sir," Ken said, turning back to regard Jimmy. "Boss," Ken said, holding up his hand. "I wasn't looking to—"

"Don't worry, Ken. I'm giving you the weekend off, and whatever I make in tips, I'll set aside for you. Seriously, you've earned it." Jimmy extended his hand. "I'm very sorry that it took me this long to acknowledge that."

"Holy fuck," Ken said, wrapping his arms around his boss. "Mindy's gonna think I got fired. She's never gonna believe we have a whole weekend together." Ken released Jimmy and turned, then stopped suddenly. "What about crowd control on Saturday, with the new band coming in?"

"I can handle it," Jimmy said, trying not to look too wounded. "Now get out of here before I change my mind." He would have said that he'd never seen Ken move that quickly, but the truth was, despite being an ex-con who was near the end of his rope less than a year before, Ken was the best employee Jimmy had ever hired.

"What can I get you?" Jimmy turned and looked at the tall, handsome man sitting at the bar.

"Nothing for me, thanks." The man nodded and took a piece of paper from his back pocket. Jimmy couldn't help but notice how the fabric of the white shirt stretched across a firm chest, the V at the neck revealing that it was probably quite hairy. "I came in here to talk to the owner, but I'm thinking now that I'd rather get to know you a little better first."

"The owner?"

"Yeah, I'll be playing here this weekend. You gonna be here, darlin'?"

"Always am."

"Well, I look forward to getting to know you better. Maybe we can do that after the show?"

Jimmy tilted his head and looked apologetic. "Sorry, darlin', but as the owner, I'll be pretty busy."

"You're Jimmy Campbell?"

Jimmy nodded. "And you are?"

The stranger extended his hand, offering his best seductive smile. Jimmy took it, reluctantly, and felt the strong, firm handshake. "Name's Derek Roberts. But with you, I'm just Dizzy."

Jimmy laughed in spite of himself and released the man's hand. "That ever work for you, Derek?"

"Dizzy, please."

"Okay, Dizzy," Jimmy said as he pointed off to his left. "Well, let me show you where you'll be playing."

"Great," the man said. "I called earlier in the week, but no one got back to me. And now I'm kind of grateful that they didn't."

"The stage is permanent, and it's a pretty big size, so you shouldn't have any problems setting up your equipment, and—"

"That's okay, darlin'. I do my best work in tight spaces."

Great. Jimmy retreated behind the bar. *It's not enough I got drunks coming on to me. Now I have to fight off some oversexed Marlboro man.* "Don't you worry your pretty little head, there, Dizzy. There'll be plenty of half-dressed gym bunnies hanging around the stage. You'll have your pick of tight spaces."

"Not really my type," Dizzy said as he moved to stand opposite Jimmy. "Nothing better than a finely tuned, seasoned instrument. Nicer sound, nicer feel, if you know what I mean."

"Yeah, I'm not having any trouble following you, there, Dizzy. Unfortunately I'm not interested. So, best you stick with those gym bunnies. If you're as good as you think you are, you should be able to have them tuned and seasoned in no time." Jimmy was suddenly regretting giving Ken the weekend off. "Anything else you need, Dizzy?" He saw the man leer and open his mouth. "Keeping in mind that a pitcher full of ice water is good at cooling things down."

The man tipped an imaginary hat and offered his hand one more time. "Not right now, darlin'. But if you're serious about coolin' me down, you're gonna need a lot more than just one pitcher."

Jimmy couldn't help but smile and found himself thinking of all the clientele who would be willing to give this man whatever he wanted. "I'll keep that in mind, Dizzy."

"The pleasure was all mine, darlin'." Dizzy walked a few steps and turned around. "Next time, maybe you'll let me return the favor."

This time, Jimmy did laugh out loud. He leaned against the bar and watched as Dizzy's long, muscular legs took him toward the exit. *God, that one's gonna be nothing but trouble.* He returned to wiping tables and taking drink orders.

Chapter 2

DIZZY WALKED out of the bar, whistling that new song to himself. He'd only written it a couple of weeks ago, and this weekend's gig would be the first chance he'd have to test it for a live crowd. And with that fine-looking man in there, Dizzy would have just the right inspiration to do the song justice.

He unlocked his SUV, climbed into the driver's seat, and turned the key. Dizzy pulled the SUV out of the parking lot and headed the few miles down the highway to his hotel, thinking about Jimmy Campbell. He knew he was grinning because he wasn't used to getting turned down like that. Since he'd divorced his wife almost fifteen years ago, Dizzy's bed was hardly ever empty. Even when he was touring with his band and staying in hotel rooms, Dizzy could always count on an evening filled with the company of a handsome man or two. But this Jimmy—he was going to require some special handling. And Dizzy was quite certain that he would definitely make it worth his while.

Although not as tall as Dizzy, Jimmy had a full head of blond hair and dazzling baby blues that got an unmistakable glint that seemed to say, "I want you, but you're going to have to work for it." These were the times when Dizzy appreciated the fact that he'd always taken care of himself. Sure, he'd always worked out and eaten healthy when he was working as a cop. But now, retired from the force, the unexpected bonus to keeping fit was Dizzy's amazing stamina. He'd have his bedmates panting and begging long before he got around to his favorite part—riding them nice and slow. And when they were screaming out his name, he'd pick up the pace—only to slow down, just to show them who was in charge. The end result was always the same: they were always very happy to see him, and he always made sure to leave them spent, sweaty, and with a huge smile on their faces.

He had a man or two in every town he'd ever played, and a very long list of telephone numbers to prove it. Dizzy had never played this town before, so he was looking forward to adding Jimmy's name to that list. And if his usual lines didn't work on Jimmy Campbell, then he'd just think up a few new ones, maybe dedicate a few songs to the man. Dizzy enjoyed a good challenge, and something told him that Jimmy would be worth it.

Dizzy felt the phone vibrate in his pocket and pulled over to the side of the highway. He quickly looked at the display and saw it was his ex-wife. He plastered a smile on his face, then punched the accept button and waited for the fireworks.

"Hello, Beth."

"Braden just called me and told me the university hasn't received the payment for this semester."

"I'm fine, thanks for asking."

"Derek, don't make me get the lawyers involved, again."

"Don't threaten me, Beth," Dizzy cautioned as his grip tightened on the phone. "Would you prefer fax or e-mail?"

"What are you talking about?"

"I can either fax or e-mail a copy of the check I sent to Braden over two months ago. Oh, and I can also send you proof that Kelley's school fees were paid as well."

"Why the fuck would you send the check to Braden?"

"Because he asked me to."

"Jesus Christ, Derek, you do realize he's probably spent the money already?"

"And how is that my problem? He's an adult now." Dizzy felt the self-satisfied smile curl his lips. He lived for these moments when Beth got her comeuppance. It was why Dizzy lived so frugally. He met all of his financial responsibilities as set out in the divorce, with military-like precision, just for these moments. "I meet all my obligations, Beth. If Braden lies to me and spends the money, that's his problem, not mine."

"And where's the money going to come from for his tuition?"

"Again, not my problem." *And now for the truth.* "I'm apparently nothing but the bank here, Beth. I'm not the one who spoiled them rotten and spent the last ten years telling them I'm a good-for-nothing faggot."

"Oh, fuck you, Derek."

"Oh, and Beth?" Dizzy didn't wait for her to respond. "Perhaps you could tell Braden to go and get a job. Oh, perhaps that man who's so much better than me might get off his ass and make his own goddamn money instead of living off mine. Interesting, isn't it? You call me good-for-nothing, when the man you claim loves you more than I ever did won't marry you because your alimony would stop." Dizzy took the phone away from his ear and looked at the screen. He waited for the invective to begin and was only slightly surprised when Beth had nothing to offer in response. He punched the button to end the call and sighed.

I met a handsome man today, with the finest ass and longest legs I've ever seen and finally managed to shut Beth up. Dizzy tossed the phone onto the passenger seat, put the SUV in gear, and made a quick U-turn back to the bar. *Pretty good day.* He saw the bar in the distance. *Let's see if I can't end it with those legs wrapped around my neck.*

Dizzy parked his SUV and turned off the engine, pocketing his keys as he jumped out and headed for the bar. He pulled the door open and breezed in with that slight swagger to his hips that always managed to draw focus to what he was packing between his legs and show off his firm ass at the same time.

Jimmy was clearing the tables, so Dizzy just propped himself against the bar and watched those legs and that ass move effortlessly around the room. There were even fewer people than had been before, but he figured that was because it was almost nine o'clock. Business probably wouldn't pick up for another few hours.

Dizzy switched his position as he saw Jimmy head back to the bar, probably to unload the tray he was carrying. He stood with his elbows on the bar, proudly showing off that firm ass so Jimmy could get a good look at one of the many breathtaking views that would be his for the night. Dizzy watched in the mirror behind the bar as Jimmy noticed him.

"You forget something?"

"Could never forget you, darlin'." Jimmy seemed to force a smile and started putting dirty glasses into the stainless steel sanitizer.

"What can I get you, Dizzy?"

"What're you offering?"

"List's right there on the wall," Jimmy said, pointing to the wall before heading to the other end of the bar to take a couple of orders.

Dizzy took a moment to appreciate the curve of the ass where it met the small of Jimmy's back. He let his eyes travel down to take in the way the jeans hugged the man's thighs. After Jimmy had placed two beers on the counter and the customers had disappeared back to their tables, Dizzy watched as Jimmy returned to stand near him. "I don't see what I want on the list."

"Let me guess," Jimmy said, forcing a smile again. "You don't see me up there, right?"

"No, darlin'," Dizzy said, his voice low and husky. "I was hoping I could get a Bud."

"That's weird," Jimmy said, turning and reaching into the fridge. "Bud's the first one on the list." He pulled out a Bud and slid it down to Dizzy. "Glass or bottle?"

"That is weird. Maybe I need glasses. Huh." Dizzy took a mouthful of beer, swallowed, pulled the bottle away from his lips, and licked them slowly. "Bottle's fine, darlin'. Thank you. How much?"

"On the house," Jimmy said as he threw the towel over his shoulder and headed back to loading the sanitizer.

"Mighty nice of you," Dizzy said, then took another mouthful of beer as he looked around the space. "Slow night or does it pick up later?"

"About normal for a Thursday," Jimmy said as he finished loading the sanitizer. "Busy after work, but crowds disappear around eight or so when they remember they gotta work tomorrow."

"How about on the weekends?"

"Busier than a one-armed paper hanger," Jimmy said, leaning against the bar. "Especially since we've started featuring live bands on Saturday nights."

"You mean I'm not your first?"

"Thought you liked 'em seasoned?" Jimmy said, smiling, probably thinking he'd scored a point or two.

"Oh, I do, but there's something to be said for new experiences. Don't you think?"

"I guess that depends on what you think you got that I haven't had before."

Dizzy laughed out loud and brought the beer up to his lips again, giving him some precious seconds to think. "Well, how about you tell me what you've had before, and I'll let you know if I got better."

"You know, now I think about it, there is one thing you could do for me that I haven't been offered in a really, really long time."

"Anything for you, darlin'." Dizzy felt a stirring in his pants and started planning his seduction. *This wasn't as hard as I thought it was gonna be.* He leaned over the bar a little more.

"How about talking to me like a grown man and treating me like I'm not only interested in what's in your pants?"

Dizzy's smile disappeared almost instantly. "Hey, look, darlin'—"

"Jimmy. My name is Jimmy. Not darlin'."

"Okay," Dizzy said, realizing just then that the man wasn't yelling or even frowning—he was smiling. "Listen, Jimmy, I'm sorry. I didn't mean nothing by it. It's just some harmless flirting."

"You ever stop to ask yourself how much harmless flirting I gotta put up with in a place like this? You ever wonder if maybe the people who turn you down might just want a sincere conversation?"

"Don't know. Never been turned down." Dizzy heard the words and saw Jimmy roll his eyes. "I'm sorry. I—"

"You mind me asking you a personal question?"

Dizzy shook his head.

"How old are you?"

"Be fifty-one in two months."

"Well, I'm forty-five. Just turned. And I've been out since I was eighteen. That's twenty-seven years of listening to that kind of crap. And there's only one thing I'm looking for right now."

"What's that?"

"A man. A man who knows how to be responsible. A man who wants to know more about me than just my phone number. A man who can recognize that 'no' might mean I've got some needs that don't involve lying on my back and telling him how big he is and how no man will ever be as good."

Dizzy watched Jimmy turn and reach into the fridge again. He pulled out another Bud and placed it on the bar. "Thank you, Jimmy." He finished his first beer and pushed it aside. He pulled the second in front of himself and played nervously with the label.

"You're welcome."

"I apologize, Jimmy." Dizzy felt his face burning slightly, as it had when he had to sit and listen to Beth and the lawyers argue over child support and visitation and betrayal. He wanted to reach out and throttle them, even his own lawyer, but he hadn't because he knew that his decision to finally come out had caused almost all of the problems. And here he was again. He'd been an ass to this nice man, who still hadn't lost his temper, and he felt like shit for doing it. "Happy belated birthday." He held up his bottle. "Can I buy you one? Can we start over?"

"No, thank you. To the beer, I mean. I don't drink. Well, not on the job, anyway. But we can most definitely start again."

Dizzy extended his hand and offered a sincere smile. "Derek Roberts. Very nice to meet you."

"Nice to meet you, Derek. Jimmy Campbell." Jimmy put his hand in Derek's.

"Okay, then, Jimmy. I've got a question for you."

"And what's that?"

"You ever free from this place? I'd love to take you out to dinner while I'm in town."

"Can't do dinner, especially this weekend."

"Okay, fair enough." Derek took another mouthful of beer. "What time are you here on Saturday?"

"Bar'll open at six, and your first set will be at eight."

"No, I meant what time will you be here, 'cause I was thinking I could bring lunch by an hour or so before the band sets up. And we could get to know each other a little better."

"I'll be here by eleven in the morning, or so."

"So? Two? Three?"

"I'll be here."

"Great," Derek said as he pushed himself away from the bar. "Anything you don't like to eat?"

"I'm vegan."

"Got it. No meat." Derek took a few steps toward the door and turned around. Jimmy was still looking at him. "It was nice talking with you, Jimmy."

"Good night, Derek."

He waved and walked out of the bar, feeling a little relieved. He wasn't sure if he was relieved because he could finally put away the routine and be himself, or because he'd just made a date with the first man who'd ever called him on his bullshit. Either way Derek figured he'd found something he hadn't had in a great many years. Derek was excited at the possibility that he'd just made a friend, a friend who would appreciate everything the real Derek had to offer.

Chapter 3

THE ALARM went off at eight o'clock, as it did every Friday. Jimmy reached over, swatted at the snooze button, and snuggled under the covers, right next to the soft fur of his two-year-old Yorkie. Jimmy inhaled deeply. The smell of Bozo's fur never failed to make him relax. Bozo stood up on the mattress and shifted his position, then lay down again so he could lick Jimmy's nose.

"Morning," Jimmy said as he felt the little paws of the Maine coon kitty he'd adopted almost two years ago. "And to you too, Miss Alicia." Jimmy rolled onto his back and patted his chest—the permission the cat was waiting for. She trotted up and stood on his T-shirt, her paws kneading for a few moments before she finally turned around and lay down with her butt right in his face. Jimmy laughed, reached up to stroke her long tail, and delighted in the loud purring that made his entire torso vibrate.

Bozo raised himself again and repositioned his little body so that his head was resting across Jimmy's neck. Jimmy closed his eyes and sighed. This wasn't the usual morning routine for the three of them. Most days the alarm would sound much later. After feeding the two of them, Jimmy would shower and shave. Then he would take Bozo out for a nice long walk while Miss Alicia stayed inside to begin her very busy day of lounging.

"Okay, babies," Jimmy said as the alarm sounded again. "It's Friday. You know what that means." Jimmy lifted his head slightly, causing Bozo to move back onto the pillow. Then he scooped Miss Alicia off his chest and placed her on the bed beside him. He got up and walked toward the kitchen, his two companions in hot pursuit. "And since it's your favorite day of the week, you know that means you get your favorite foods."

Jimmy opened a can of tuna for Miss Alicia, dumped it into a bowl, and placed it on the floor beside her water bowl. While she gently defended her bowl from her inquisitive brother, Jimmy opened the fridge to retrieve the cut up cubes of chicken he'd prepared the night before and added them to Bozo's usual kibble. He barely got the bowl on the ground before Bozo started licking his hand.

As he headed to the shower, Jimmy turned to take a final look at his fur-babies. He'd certainly lucked out when he found these two at the city shelter. The two of them went for him right away, not wasting any time at all before licking his hand and letting him pet them through the cages. He hadn't been surprised at the friendliness of the Yorkie, but he had been taken aback by Miss Alicia coming to him right away, especially after the shelter worker had explained that the cat had been there for almost a year. The worker described Miss Alicia as never being mean or aggressive with the other animals or with any of the potential adopters, but rather being aloof and reserved.

After he got the two animals home, it hadn't taken Jimmy too long to realize that she was not aloof or reserved. She was a true lady. She and Bozo had never fought over anything or showed even the slightest aggression to each other. He'd kept the name that the shelter had given Bozo, but had decided to change the cat's name. It brought Jimmy back to the time when a young girl had given him hope, had made him feel that everything would be okay again. That girl's name had been Alicia. In her honor Miss Kitty had become Miss Alicia. Even with the rambunctious Bozo, Miss Alicia was kind and patient, just as the young girl had been with Jimmy. Despite what his young friend had been going through, she always managed to make Jimmy laugh—to see the world as a gift. Just like Bozo and Miss Alicia had done since he'd brought them home. Jimmy eventually decided to register them as therapy animals.

Even on days like today, when they would spend most of the morning visiting sick children and a few of the geriatric residents at the hospital, Jimmy's companions remained patient. They instinctively knew they were there to provide hope and comfort. Jimmy had even been contacted by a nurse at one of the senior homes on the outskirts of the city. Her husband had been a patient at the hospital, and she'd heard wonderful things about his visits. She'd spoken with the home's director and set up a test visit to see if the residents might like some four-legged companionship.

In less than a year, Jimmy had two certified therapy animals and spent every Friday visiting the hospital. He'd thought that just having the animals would be a great way to relax and keep himself active, but he found that his visits to the hospitals did him even more good.

And the animals loved the attention, especially Bozo. He'd usually leave with ribbons or braids in his hair and an entire ward filled with new friends who couldn't wait to see him again. And Miss Alicia did wonders for not only the children, but the geriatric patients as well. She would lay beside them and purr up a storm while they caressed her soft fur and told her how much she reminded them of their own pets or the strays they used to feed when they were youngsters.

"Okay, babies," Jimmy said, coming out of the bathroom and pushing his damp hair out of his eyes. "Time to go visit the kiddies." He pulled the carriers out of the hall closet and opened them, knowing that they would each find their way when they finished eating. He returned to the bedroom and tossed the towel on the bed before getting dressed in his jeans and a simple green T-shirt.

"Pick your toy," Jimmy said as he stood behind the carriers. He watched as Bozo couldn't seem to make up his mind. He remembered the envelope on the table and hurried to retrieve it. When he returned to the carriers, he wasn't surprised to see Bozo making several trips between the carrier and his toy box. "No, Bozo, only one toy. You know the rules." The toys were for the ride in the car. With her usual calm and serene approach to everything, Miss Alicia did not have a problem with the drive, but Bozo was a completely different story. He spent most of the twenty-minute drive whimpering and whining. He associated car rides with being able to stick his muzzle out the window and bark at the wind or try to catch snowflakes on his tongue in the winter. But when they were heading to the hospital, Jimmy kept them both in their carriers to avoid any potential accidents and to keep them from getting dirty. The hospital had very strict rules about just how clean the animals had to be.

Jimmy moved the carriers to the hall, locked the door to his upstairs apartment, and headed down the outside stairs to the car. He stowed the carriers in the backseat and then hopped into the driver's seat. Within minutes they were on their way to the hospital. He patted the envelope in his pocket. There were two checks in this year's envelope. The first check was his usual yearly donation. Although he always requested they spend the donations on the children, he never bothered to ask. They'd spend the money whichever way they felt best, and that was good enough for him. The other check was meant for one specific family. He wondered briefly if Bozo would notice that one of his usual companions was absent. He took a deep breath to avoid showing up with tears in his eyes and focused on letting his fur-babies work their magic yet again.

"Here we are, babies," Jimmy announced as he pulled into the parking lot of the hospital. He parked as far away as possible, not wanting to take up a closer stall. He had no problem walking, so why should he park closer and deprive someone who might? He made it to the door, walked inside, and greeted the guards and the receptionist. Sheila, his usual contact, was just getting off the elevator.

"Hello, Jimmy. They've been asking about you."

"Hi, Sheila. I'm not late, am I?"

"No, but you know that doesn't matter." Sheila laughed and escorted him to the elevator and got on as soon as Jimmy had the animals safely inside. "Little Kyle, new patient, woke up at six this morning and started asking when Bozo was coming. I asked him how he even knew about that. Apparently some of the other kids told him all about Friday mornings."

"I don't wanna know," Jimmy said, feeling that familiar burning behind his eyes. "Honestly, Sheila, I don't know how you do this day after day."

"You get used to it, I guess." Sheila must have sensed something in Jimmy's expression. "Not the dying or the parents outliving their kids part. I just mean you learn to deal with it in a way that doesn't destroy your desire to make a difference."

"Speaking of which," Jimmy said as he set the carriers down. He reached into his pocket and pulled out the envelope. "Usual donation, and there's a special something in there for Josh's parents. I know they can't afford a funeral, so I wanted to lighten that particular burden for them."

"Jimmy," Sheila sighed. "I know you wanna help everyone, but you keep giving your money away, you're gonna lose your bar and your home. And then what will we do without Bozo and Miss Alicia, huh?"

"Money's not a big worry for me, Sheila." He was anxious to change the subject. "Will you give it to them, and keep my name out of it, please?"

"But if it's a check—"

"Bank draft, made out to both parents. It's certified so that they won't have any problems cashing it."

"Okay," Sheila said, looking at the envelope and shaking her head. "How the hell are you still single?"

Jimmy laughed, knowing she meant it rhetorically. "'Cause you keep saying no, that's why."

Sheila put the envelope in the pocket of her uniform and slapped playfully at Jimmy's shoulder. "Now you, you stop teasing an old woman."

"Old, right," Jimmy said, his voice dripping with disbelief. "You're only ten years older than I am."

Sheila's face broke into a broad grin as she regarded Jimmy for a moment. "Ten years? Okay, either I lied to you when I told you my age, or you're adding a couple of decades to your own to make me feel better."

The elevator's chime sounded, and the doors whooshed open. Jimmy stooped to pick up the carriers and then followed Sheila to the nurse's station. Bozo would lead him to the children while Miss Alicia stayed in her carrier so her paws wouldn't slip and slide on the shiny floors.

As he headed north, Jimmy smiled at the little cooing noises Sheila was making to Bozo. Soon enough he heard the click-clack of Bozo's newly trimmed nails on the spotless floor. Just before he was out of earshot, Jimmy heard the chorus of young voices calling out in unison, "Bozo!"

He smiled and walked into Mrs. Abramovich's room.

"Good morning, Mrs. Abramovich," Jimmy called in a singsong voice. "Miss Alicia insisted on coming in here first."

Jimmy opened the carrier at the foot of the woman's bed and watched, spellbound as always. The docile cat stretched for a moment and then ambled her way up to lick Mrs. Abramovich's hand and finally settled down beside her arm and did what she always did best—purr up a storm. "I'll let you two visit," Jimmy said, stowing the carrier under the bed before heading down to see the children.

During a brief stay in the hospital when he was nineteen years old, Jimmy had found great comfort in talking with Alicia, a girl he'd met in the courtyard. They talked about their plans for the future and all the things they were going to do when they got out. Jimmy looked forward to their chats. They made him feel normal again—like he hadn't just lived through a nervous breakdown. Talking to Alicia had helped Jimmy figure out why he'd been so unhappy that he'd wound up in the hospital.

They made plans to meet when they got out of the hospital and to remain friends, no matter what. But Alicia had never gotten out. She died there, just short of her seventeenth birthday. Jimmy visited with her at least once a week, and despite her deteriorating appearance, he convinced himself that he would not lose his new friend. *We'll be a hundred years old and in rocking chairs. You'll see.* Alicia would just smile weakly and tell him she would always be with him. All he had to do was say her name, and she would come to him.

As he entered the children's ward to the sound of laughter, Jimmy thanked Alicia for everything she'd done for him. Again.

Chapter 4

JIMMY HAD finished sweeping only half the floor in the bar when he heard the knock at the front entrance. Bozo's head popped up from his temporary bed in the corner, but he didn't bark. Jimmy checked the clock over the bar and saw that it was already two in the afternoon. As he walked to the door to greet Derek, Jimmy wondered where the time had gone. It seemed like only minutes since he'd been walking Bozo outside, returned home to play with him and Miss Alicia, and settled in with them for their usual Saturday midmorning nap. Of course, Miss Alicia was prone to her beauty naps during the day, so Jimmy had Bozo with him, so they wouldn't disturb her.

As Jimmy opened the door for Derek, whose hands were filled with plastic bags, Bozo slowly trotted over, ever the faithful guard dog. Jimmy took some of the bags, placed them on the bar, and turned back for the others—only to stop at the sight of Bozo on his back getting belly rubs from a complete stranger.

"He's such a sweetie," Derek said, grinning at Bozo's antics. "He hasn't even barked once."

"That's Bozo," Jimmy sighed as he walked over and retrieved the remaining bags. "He's very used to being the center of attention."

"I can see why," Derek said as he picked up Bozo and cradled him in his arms. "Have you had him long? Looks like he's what? Two or three?"

"Two. Good eye." Jimmy moved behind the bar and searched for plates and cutlery, then turned his attention to unpacking the bags. "Is your band coming too? How many people are you feeding?"

"Sorry," Derek said as he put Bozo back on the floor. "Wasn't sure what you'd like, so I just got some of everything. Besides, if there are any leftovers, maybe I can wrangle an invite for tomorrow too."

Jimmy stopped opening cartons and containers and took a deep breath. "Listen, Derek. I'd like to apologize for saying those things to you on Thursday. I—"

"No! Stop right there," Derek said. He winked and held up his left hand. "I deserved it. I should be apologizing to you." Derek began helping Jimmy organize their lunchtime feast. "Truth is, I've been kind of on a wild streak for far too many years. Got kind of addicted to the attention from all the fans and figured the only thing I needed to do to win you over was to try a little harder."

"Believe it or not, I understand."

"Oh ho," Derek said and whistled. "So I'm not the only one who could feed a country with the wild oats he's sowed, huh?"

"No, nothing like that. Just meant that I know what it feels like to have people filling your head with all sorts of nonsense just because they want something else from you." Jimmy put the plates on the counter of the bar and turned to the fridges behind him. "What would you like to drink?"

"Check that bag there," Derek said as he opened the last plastic container.

Jimmy did as he was told and found a selection of wine, beer, and nonalcoholic drinks. "What's all this? You hit fifty and your memory's shot? You remembered you were having lunch in a bar, right? What's with all the drinks?"

"Sorry, sonny, could you speak up?" Derek said as he hunched over and walked a few steps as if he were a frail old man. "I'm in a hurry, you see. Got some courtin' to do with this young fella what owns a bar."

Jimmy shook his head and deposited the bag of drinks in the fridge, then pulled out a cold Bud for Derek and an iced tea for himself.

"Didn't want to presume, that's all. I'm an old-fashioned kind of guy. If I ask you out on a date, I think ahead, plan, put some effort into it."

"Well, this is a very nice treat. Thank you, Derek." Jimmy decided to try a compliment instead of asking Derek just how much planning had ever gone into his endless series of one-night stands and booty calls.

"I know I sound like a hypocrite, but you made it clear that you wanted a man. A responsible man who knows that 'no' means you've got other needs besides what's in my pants." Derek stopped and watched as Jimmy filled his plate with a few scoops from each container. Jimmy knew that this food wasn't completely vegan, what with the cream sauces and diced eggs in the potato salad, but he had to commend Derek for a good effort. He finished loading his plate and handed a napkin to Derek.

"I came out a little late, and my marriage before that was…. Well, let's just say it wasn't satisfying. Anyway, I see a fine-looking man such as yourself, and all I can think about is making up for a lot of lost time," Derek said.

Jimmy waited for Derek to load his own plate and then led him to one of the tables. "Well, I'm sorry for being rude." Jimmy noticed Derek rush to put his plate on the table and then come around to pull out the chair for him. "And just for your information, this Derek who's here right now, he'll get me in bed a helluva lot faster than Dizzy. If Dizzy could at all." Jimmy smiled at the expression on Derek's ruggedly handsome face.

Derek coughed and returned to his side of the table. "I'll, uh, keep that in mind." He twisted the cap of his Bud, grinned, and raised the bottle. "To second chances."

Jimmy picked up his iced tea and touched the side of Derek's beer bottle. "Mind if I ask about you being married? Or is that something you don't wanna talk about?"

"No, don't mind." Derek took a mouthful of beer and picked up his fork. "I was thirty and still single, working as a cop—"

"That explains it."

"Explains what?"

"The rugged good looks, the great physique." Jimmy offered a lopsided grin, delighting in the slow blush over Derek's fair skin. "Or is that just my fantasy?"

"Wow," Derek said, taking another mouthful of beer. "When you flirt, you don't mess around, do you?"

"That was just a compliment," Jimmy said, raising an eyebrow. "When I flirt with you, you'll know it 'cause your pants will feel awful snug." Jimmy winked and leaned on the edge of the table. "Thirty years old and single. Keep going."

"I was still single and had spent too many years convincing myself I was straight. Met Beth at a friend's wedding, and it seemed like we wanted the same things. But, turns out, we didn't." Derek took a bite of his club sandwich and shook his head, chewing quickly. "I mean besides the obvious. She wanted kids, and I wasn't sure, but figured it was just something married folk do." As if sensing he was needed, Bozo ambled over and waited at Derek's feet. "You mind?"

"No, not at all. Chicken is his favorite," Jimmy said around a mouthful of salad. "Bacon works well too," he added, pointing at Derek's club sandwich. Jimmy couldn't help but smile as he watched Derek break off pieces of bacon and feed them to Bozo. "You've made a friend for life."

"Never have too many of those."

"Ain't that the truth," Jimmy said, realizing that there was a life story contained in Derek's sentence. Jimmy decided to get back to the subject. "How many kids do you have?"

"Two. Boy who's nineteen and a girl, seventeen." Derek looked up. For the first time, Jimmy saw that there was quite a bit of hurt lurking behind the flirtatious grin and devil-may-care attitude. "I tried to hang in there as long as I could, for the kids, I mean, but...." Derek lowered his head, shaking it slowly. "But it finally dawned on me that the damage had been done, and nothing I could do or say would change that."

"Do you see them? The kids, not Beth." Jimmy chewed his food slowly as he studied Derek's face.

"No," Derek sighed, feeding Bozo some more bacon. "I still keep trying, but they don't want anything to do with their old man."

"I'm sorry, Derek. We can talk about something else if you'd like."

"'S okay, darlin'. Sorry, Jimmy." Derek offered a fragile smile. "Spent the last ten years trying to figure out how I can fix it, but I think I finally figured out that the whole mess isn't mine to fix."

"Good for you." Jimmy picked up his iced tea. "Darlin'."

"What about you? What's your tragic tale?"

"Not much to tell, really. Been the owner of this bar since I was in my midtwenties. Like to do volunteer work around town when I'm not here—"

"No, I meant what's your story when it comes to romance. A handsome man like you? Can't believe you're still single."

"Well, I am." Jimmy went back to finishing his lunch, not really wanting to tell Derek anything about his past. Perhaps one day, but not now. "Guess I just never found the right man."

"They do seem to be in short supply, don't they?"

"So, you were a cop but now you're in a band, touring and playing in honky-tonks like mine."

"Yeah, pretty much. And this ain't no honky-tonk. This is one of the nicest bars I've seen in a long time."

"Thank you. Much appreciated." Bozo decided to try his luck with Jimmy. He sat up and looked hopeful. Jimmy took a few tomato pieces, held them out for Bozo to sniff, and was quite surprised when he gulped them down. "Hmmm, I guess I should see if he'll eat other vegetables."

"Tomato isn't necessarily bad for your dog, but they are in the nightshade family, so I never let my dogs eat them. Try the carrots. Those are totally safe."

Jimmy jumped off his stool and retrieved the uneaten tomato pieces, then put down a few carrot slices when Bozo looked confused. "Thank you, Derek. Wait? Where do your dogs stay when you're on the road?" Jimmy slid back onto his stool, his eyes focused on the sad expression on Derek's face.

"Don't have one right now. I've only had three. When I was a boy, I had a Boxer named Casey. Got him when I was five and had him until I was twenty-two. And after Casey I rescued a Saint Bernard who was already six when we found each other. Named him Bernie." Jimmy couldn't help but notice the twinkle in Derek's eyes as he remembered his dogs. "And then there was Max, short for Maximum, because that boy loved to do everything as hard and as fast as he could."

"Was he a Saint Bernard, as well?"

"No, Max was a Chihuahua. He was thirteen when I saw him on a website. I'd just left the force and Beth and the kids. Max went everywhere with me. But within a few years, he wasn't doing so well.

Turned out to be kidney failure. Stopped touring to take care of him, but eventually had to let him go."

Jimmy tried to imagine the day when he'd have to say good-bye to his two babies. He reached across and put his hand over Derek's. "I'm so sorry."

"Never understood how people could just abandon animals 'cause they got old." Derek picked up Jimmy's hand and kissed it. He waved his hand in the air. "But you didn't invite me here for a lecture about responsible pet ownership."

"I've always been one of those crazy people who believes that we don't rescue the animals, they rescue us."

"Yeah," Derek said, turning his hand so he could hold onto Jimmy's. He gave it a quick squeeze. "Me too. It was a very lonely time for me, starting all over again like that."

"Scary too, I'd imagine?"

"Yes. Scary too." Derek took a long drag on his beer and looked at Jimmy. "Sound like you lived through some hard times as well."

Jimmy nodded slowly. "Been on my own since I was seventeen."

"No family? At all?"

Jimmy shook his head, wondering how much information he should be sharing with this man. He was serious when he said that Derek would be able to bed him faster than the obnoxiously cocky Dizzy, but this man was on the road all the time. What kind of future could Jimmy hope to have with a long-distance relationship when the distance between them would not even be consistent from one week to the next?

"Listen, Jimmy," Derek said, his voice a mere whisper. "I was wondering if you might like a pen pal."

"A pen pal?"

"Gets awfully lonely on the road sometimes." Derek blushed and shook his head. "I'm not talking about just the sex. Sure, I get plenty of action. But that's all it ever is. It's just sex, and I don't think any of them really give a shit about listening to me talk about my kids or my dogs." Derek stopped for a moment, tilted his head to one side, and waved his hand in front of his face. "Sorry, I don't really know what I was thinking."

"How would I get my letters to you?"

Derek smiled and looked into Jimmy's eyes. "You could e-mail me, you know, since you won't always have an address."

Jimmy returned Derek's smile. "Okay," he said, getting off his stool and retrieving a pen and paper from the bar. He could feel Derek's eyes traveling up and down his body. He wrote out the information and then walked back to stand in front of Derek, folding the piece of paper. "When do you leave for your next gig?"

"Monday morning."

"Any idea when you'll be back this way?"

"Be another month or so, I imagine."

Jimmy tucked the piece of paper into Derek's shirt pocket, leaning in as he did so. He saw the confusion on Derek's face as he brought their lips together. Derek rested his hands on Jimmy's hips, his legs parted to allow him to get even closer. Jimmy wrapped his arms around the back of Derek's strong neck and allowed his tongue to push gently against Derek's full lips. Their tongues touched tentatively at first, then eagerly as they began to move and explore with their hands. Jimmy could hear the sounds of their moans, their hands rubbing against clothing, and their heavy breathing. When he needed air, he pulled away and stared into Derek's eyes. "Monday morning, huh? You free Sunday night?"

"Not anymore," Derek said, releasing his hold on Jimmy.

"How about I make you a nice home-cooked dinner on Sunday?"

"Can't really think of anything else I'd rather do, to tell you the truth."

Chapter 5

DEREK SAT on the sofa in Jimmy's upstairs apartment. Miss Alicia sat on his lap, purring louder than anything he'd ever heard. Bozo was snoozing in the pet bed on the floor at the end of the sofa. Derek had another hour or so before he had to go on with the rest of the band. They arrived shortly after Jimmy had surprised the hell out of him with that mind-blowing kiss. Derek felt as if he'd been sucker-punched.

"Dizzy?"

He carefully moved Miss Alicia when he heard one of his bandmates. "Yeah, right here." He stood up and went to meet Clark. "What's up?"

"Nothing. Jimmy said we could hang out up here until we go on." Clark walked into the apartment and looked around. "He is some fine piece of ass, huh? Wish I had one of him in every town we played."

"You get plenty of action, Clark, especially for a man who'd fit right in at a pig's trough."

"Fuck, man. It's not like you haven't done the same thing."

"And when's the last time you ever heard me talk about any of them like that? The man's been kind enough to let us into his apartment, and you disrespect him like that?"

"Relax, Diz," Clark said, his grin becoming broader. "Oh, I get it. He's yours, that it?"

Derek opened his mouth to tell Clark to leave Jimmy alone but then thought twice. "You know what, Clark? You want him? You give it your best shot."

"Yeah?"

"And if you do manage to fuck him, I'll let you try out that song you think is so good."

"Deal," Clark said, holding out his hand for a gentleman's agreement.

Derek shook his hand and grinned, knowing full well what kind of experience Clark was in for. He watched Clark straighten his T-shirt, puff out his chest, and then leave the apartment. Derek figured he was heading down to work his magic, and he didn't want to miss a second's worth of the entertainment. He closed the door to the apartment and reminded himself to tell Jimmy he'd need to run up and lock it.

As he headed into the bar, he grabbed Phil and Nick, the other two members of the band. He filled them in on the upcoming fireworks and took a seat at the end of the bar.

"This is gonna be good," Phil, the bassist, said as he stood beside Derek. "I swear that guy gets lucky once and it's enough encouragement for the next hundred rejections."

"He's good-looking enough," Derek said, shrugging his shoulders. "But he really needs to work on his pickup lines."

"Funny," Phil said, punching Derek on the shoulder. "He says the same thing about you."

"My record stands for itself."

"Speaking of which. Was I sensing something more than your usual one-nighter when I walked in on you and Jimmy?"

"He's something special. Yeah," Derek said, watching as Jimmy leaned in to take Clark's order. When Jimmy's head reared back in a hearty laugh, Derek panicked. If it hadn't been for Phil's hand on his shoulder, Derek might have gone over to knock Clark on his ass.

Jimmy was suddenly walking over to Derek, shaking his head. "Did you put him up to this? Is this payback for bitching you out about your pickup lines?"

Derek felt like he would pass out from the relief he felt. He slowly shook his head and shrugged his shoulders again. "Go easy on him, though."

Jimmy didn't look convinced but picked up the empties at the end of the bar and quickly returned with two Buds—one for Derek and one for Phil.

"What did he say?" Derek asked, after putting his hand on Jimmy's forearm. "I mean, if you don't mind my asking."

"'How about I buy you a milk and you can do my body good?'" Jimmy stood there, his face implacable, a hand on his hip.

Derek's eyes widened as he turned to look at Phil. Both men burst into laughter at the same time. Jimmy rolled his eyes and walked back to Clark's end of the bar. Phil was wiping at the tears streaming down his face.

"Hey, calm down," Derek said as he helped prop up the bassist. "You'll get the hiccups again."

"Ah, I'm sorry," Phil said, taking the stool next to Derek. "Milk. Oh man, I ain't never gonna get tired of throwing that in his face."

"Let's go easy on him, huh? He's only twenty-seven."

"And that's old enough to know better."

"Come on," Derek said as they headed to the storage room at the back of the bar, where they heard Nick warming up. They joined him and shared Clark's latest rejection.

Nick, for his part, being around the same age as Phil and Derek, shook his head and sighed. After a few minutes, he stopped playing. "Man, I had some serious fuck-ups when I was his age."

Me too. Derek did scales on an imaginary keyboard.

Clark entered the back room and reached for his drumsticks. Derek said nothing and was relieved that neither Nick nor Phil seemed ready to begin the ribbing so soon.

"Milk?" Phil asked and almost collapsed with laughter. "Jesus H. Christ, Clark. What the hell were you thinking?"

"Fuck you, you old queen. At least I'm out there, trying. What are you doing?" Clark held his hands out in front of him, as if he were reading a book. "Oh, no, I prefer reading. I don't find any value in fucking a different guy every night." Clark was trying to imitate Phil's usual retort when any of them suggested cruising for easy one-night stands. "You don't find any value in different guys, or they don't find any value in you?"

"Good one, Clark," Phil said, holding out his hand. "Congratulations. Tell me, did that take the sting out of being laughed at, or maybe you'd like to go after my bald spot too."

"Fuck you, Phil."

"Both of you shut your fuckin' mouths." All three of them turned to look at Nick. "Both of you know you're not in kindergarten anymore, so how about you stop acting like it, huh? Besides, you don't see the way that man looks at Dizzy?"

"You fuckin' liar," Clark said, staring at Derek. "You let me go in there knowing he would shoot me down?"

"What the hell you want from me, Clark? I never told you I wasn't interested in him. I was trying to make a point about the way you were talking about the man." Derek got up from sitting on the keg of beer and moved to stand beside Clark. "Say what you want about me and my past of fucking anything that breathes, but that man is way out of my league *and* yours. He's got a helluva lot more class than me."

Derek walked out of the storage room and nearly walked right into Jimmy.

"I just came to apologize to Clark."

"Not necessary," Derek said, placing a hand on Jimmy's toned shoulder. "It's all good." Derek moved past Jimmy, not sure if he would be able to control himself if he stayed too close.

"If you're sure?"

Derek turned and nodded. "We up?"

"Fifteen minutes," Jimmy said. He moved past him and let a hand trail across Derek's belly. "I'll get Jill to introduce you."

Derek didn't know who Jill was and didn't really care. His stomach felt as if it were filled with carnivorous butterflies. He didn't know if it was because of the upcoming performance or because he would be near Jimmy as often as he could over the next two days. Derek had come to feel safer thinking of his liaisons as just fucking, but Jimmy was too classy to be thought of in those terms. In fact it was causing him some serious anxiety to realize that he could fall hard for this guy.

DEREK SPOKE into the microphone. "Before we head off for the night, folks, we got one last song for you. We don't normally do covers, but I wanted to do this one for all of you who've found all that heaven will allow."

Jimmy heard the hoots and hollers as he filled drink orders at the bar. He smiled as he listened to all the attention Derek and the band were getting. Jimmy hadn't expected much from the band, thinking they would be like a lot of bands that came through the bar. But he had to admit that Derek's raspy, sexy vocals, combined with the tight harmonies from Phil's tenor had kept the crowd drinking and dancing for two hours.

Billy had even shown up with his man, and the two of them seemed glued to each other all night. Jimmy caught the sheepish glances that Billy gave him—an apology, he figured. He smiled and even sent them a round of drinks on the house. He was happy for Billy. Perhaps this would be the first of many attempts on Billy's part to stop drinking so much and spend more time with his man—a man he obviously adored.

There was a lull in the drink orders, so Jimmy took a moment to relax and listen. Derek was glancing at him as he sang about trying to convince a bouncer to let him in because he had a date with all that heaven would allow. As he sang the song, Derek's looks got bolder, his eyes more playful until, with only a few phrases left in the song, Derek was just staring at him. *Lord, help me.* Jimmy found himself falling under the spell of Derek's many charms.

As the song ended, the crowd cheered and called for an encore. Jimmy was mixing and serving more drinks. He thought briefly of Ken, who loved this honky-tonk country music, and tried to find him and his wife, Mindy, in the crowd. Ken had come up a few times and offered to help, but Jimmy shooed him away and reminded him that he'd been doing this job for years before Ken was even born. And when that didn't do it, Jimmy reminded him that Mindy would tear both of them a new one if Ken even thought of stepping behind the bar.

"Hey, Boss. We're heading out." Ken was in front of him with his arm around his wife, a petite brunette. Jimmy had liked her from the moment he met her. She'd stood by her husband. And even though Jimmy didn't really know what that felt like—from anyone other than his employees and his pets—he had to respect anyone who would show that kind of devotion and support.

"Hey, you two have fun tonight?" Jimmy saw their smiles and figured that was answer enough. "Remember," he said to Ken. "You're not back here until Monday. Got it?" Ken nodded, and Mindy smiled and leaned over the bar to offer her thanks with a quick peck on the cheek. "My pleasure, sweetie," Jimmy said and pointed to Ken. "Now you go and have some fun."

He went back to serving drinks and was bent over, rooting through the fridge for two Millers, when he felt a hand at the small of his back. The hand slipped around his waist as he stood up. He was looking at Derek's perfect teeth and sweaty face. "Need any help?"

"No," Jimmy replied, twisting the cap of one beer and then the other. "You go and enjoy the attention. It'll be last call soon."

"Yes, sir," Derek said with a salute. He walked backward as he continued to stare at Jimmy with that lusty grin—until he bumped into the sanitizer. Then he disappeared into the crowd, but his eyes found Jimmy's every so often.

Chapter 6

"I BET you're hoping for more handouts, aren't you?" Jimmy looked down at Bozo's pleading eyes. They made Jimmy feel like he hadn't fed the dog in a month of Sundays. "Okay, Mr. Puppy-Dog Eyes. Here you go." Jimmy put a cube of chicken into Bozo's bowl and laughed as the pink tongue tickled his hand. "Even though I know you'll get more from Derek."

He went back to preparing dinner, placing tin foil over the roasted chicken and turning his attention to the potatoes, which he cut into quarters and smothered in his special mixture of olive oil and spices. He was just tossing them in a big stainless steel mixing bowl when he heard his cell phone ring. He reached for the dishtowel and wiped his hands, then moved quickly to the end of the counter.

"Hello?"

"Hi, it's me," Derek said.

"What's wrong?"

"Wrong? Nothing. I'm downstairs. I know I'm early, but I was driving Phil crazy at the hotel, so… he kicked me out."

Jimmy laughed as he headed to the door to his upstairs apartment. "I'm coming down right now to let you in."

"Okay."

Jimmy took the stairs two at a time, slowing down near the bottom because he didn't want to seem too eager. *Who am I kidding?* He jogged the forty or fifty feet to the bar's main entrance and unlocked and opened the door. "I should have told you to come to the door on the side," Jimmy said. He let Derek pass and noticed that Derek was clean-shaven and left an intoxicating musky smell in his wake. Jimmy locked the door and turned to find Derek standing very close to him, a smile on his handsome face.

"Here," Derek said after a moment. "It's dessert. For us and for Bozo."

"Good thing Miss Alicia isn't the jealous type," Jimmy said as he took the bag from Derek's hand. He caught the look of confusion. "Miss Alicia is a Maine coon. I hope you're not allergic."

"No," Derek said quickly. "I didn't think. I'm sorry, but I didn't bring anything for a cat."

"No problem," Jimmy said, pointing the way to the back stairs. He felt foolish, since Derek and his bandmates had already been in his apartment and knew the way. "She's a lady. You won't hear her complain."

"I promise I'll make it up to her." Derek crossed his hand over his heart.

"It's not a problem, really," Jimmy said, laughing at how earnest Derek looked and how determined he seemed to want to impress. "I hope you don't mind that she'll spend most of the evening in your lap."

Derek stopped walking and looked at Jimmy through narrowed eyes. He opened his mouth, shut it again, and then follow Jimmy up the stairs. "Did I pass?"

"Sorry?"

They reached the top of the stairs, and Jimmy turned the knob on the door, opened it, and once again stood aside to let Derek by.

"You mentioned Miss Alicia being in my lap all night." Derek entered the apartment and looked down to remove his shoes. "I was just wondering if you were testing me to see if I might say something about wanting something else in my lap."

"No," Jimmy said, finally understanding the attempt at humor. "No test." He smiled at Derek and motioned to the end of the hall. "Please, make yourself at home." Bozo came running around the corner, licking his chops. "You remember Bozo."

"Of course," Derek said as he crouched down and called the dog.

Jimmy wasn't surprised that Bozo made a beeline for Derek. He had an uncanny ability to remember anyone who gave him treats.

"Wow," Derek said, standing up and closing his eyes. "Whatever you're making for dinner smells like I'm back at grandma's house. I loved grandma's cooking."

"Thank you," Jimmy said, moving ahead of Derek when he didn't move right away. "We'll eat as soon as the potatoes are ready." Jimmy took the bag and moved toward the kitchen. Bozo was in hot pursuit and made a valiant effort to keep up with the bag while trying to walk on his hind legs so he could keep sniffing. "What would you like to drink?"

"I'm driving, so anything nonalcoholic will do just fine."

Jimmy saw something out of the corner of his eye and saw Derek's big hands scoop up Bozo. The two of them disappeared into the living room.

"Okay," Jimmy said, placing the bag on the counter and moving to the fridge. "I have bottled water, iced tea, root beer, ginger ale, and orange juice," Jimmy yelled from the kitchen and cocked his ear for the response.

"Iced tea is fine," Derek yelled back.

Jimmy poured the iced tea into a glass, scooped up the little plate of cheeses and assorted crackers and the iced tea, and headed back to where Derek was perched on the sofa. Miss Alicia was already in his lap, and Bozo lay beside him. "Ah, I see you've already met Miss Alicia."

"She's a big girl, huh?" Derek was stroking her fur and trying to keep his other hand away from her curious tongue. "I'm afraid I don't know much about cats."

"Maine coons are usually a little larger than your average cat, but Miss Alicia is very gentle. She'll sit on you and purr all day long if you let her." Jimmy put the iced tea on the coffee table in front of Derek and took a seat at the other end of the sofa. "She won't be offended if you move her."

"Nah, it's okay," Derek said as he reached for his iced tea and raised it toward Jimmy. "Thank you, Jimmy."

Jimmy watched as he took a sip and placed the glass back on the coffee table.

"It's quite hypnotic, isn't it? The purring, I mean."

"Very much so," Jimmy laughed as he pushed himself off the sofa. "Never fails to put me to sleep every night. Excuse me. I'm just going to put the potatoes in the oven." While he was there, he checked on the chicken as well. Everything would be ready as planned.

DEREK SHIFTED on the sofa. His lap began to feel uncomfortably warm. Images of a sweat-soaked denim crotch made him panic a little until Jimmy returned, scooped up the cat, and placed her on the sofa beside Bozo, who had fallen fast asleep.

"I know how hot it can get with her on your lap for too long," Jimmy said, blushing a little as he took a seat on the other side of the animals.

Derek wasn't sure if it was the innuendo in his comments or the fact that Jimmy had his hands so close to his crotch that made him flush, but Derek didn't really care. He was feeling a little too comfortable at that moment—enjoying the smells from the kitchen, being alone with a beautiful, sexy man who was as kind as he was generous, and having easy conversation. It was the well-ordered, contented life Derek had thought he would have with Beth—the kind of life that made four walls and a roof a refuge instead of a prison.

"So," Jimmy said after a moment or two. "Where are you off to for your next gig?"

"Clairville," Derek said, wondering if Jimmy knew where that was.

"That'll be quite a drive," Jimmy said, his eyes wide.

"No doubt about that."

"Well," Jimmy said as he petted the cat. "You have my address… and phone number."

Derek smiled. His heart felt as if it would beat out of his chest all of a sudden. "I promise not to overdo it."

"Don't be silly," Jimmy said, returning the smile. "It must get very lonely on the road like that." Jimmy took a breath. "I mean, I know you have your groupies, and you have the rest of the band, but still."

"Can I ask you about the name of the bar?" Derek didn't really want to talk about just how lonely he felt sometimes on the road. He wanted to know more about Jimmy.

"'The Afterlife'?" Jimmy continued to stroke the cat, and Derek was sure this was the loudest purring he'd ever heard from a cat. "I lost my mother when I was eight, and then my father passed away when I was twenty," Jimmy said. He took a breath and sighed.

"I'm sorry."

"Thank you," Jimmy said with a smile. "I was working as a waiter in another bar across town, and then one day I realized that if I sold the house, which my father had left me in his will, I could buy my own bar. So, the name just sort of fit, in a lot of different ways, I guess."

"Good for you," Derek said, looking down all of a sudden when Bozo's head popped up. "And you still find time to do volunteer work?"

"It's not that hard, really. After twenty years, it sort of runs itself." Jimmy's head turned as the kitchen timer sounded. "Okay," he said, scooping Miss Alicia off his lap. "Give me a couple of minutes to get everything set up, and we'll eat."

"Sounds good," Derek said, reaching down to rub Bozo's belly. "Bozo's not a big fan of licking, is he?"

"No," Jimmy yelled from the kitchen. "We trained that out of him, otherwise he wouldn't be allowed to work as a therapy dog."

"Therapy dog?"

"Bozo and Miss Alicia are both therapy animals," Jimmy said, sticking his head around the corner for a moment. "Sorry, thought I mentioned that."

Derek stood up, followed closely by Bozo, and moved to stand by the counter. "So, they do what, exactly? They go to old folks' homes and hospitals and such?"

"Yes," Jimmy said as he loaded bowls and dishes with potatoes and vegetables and placed the chicken on a platter. "Bozo is a big hit with the children... well most of them. And Miss Alicia likes to spend her time with the elderly patients."

"Wow, that's really something," Derek said, offering a low whistle. "That's amazing."

Jimmy looked up as he picked up the platter. "Dinner is served." He placed the platter on the table and then returned to the counter to retrieve the bread basket, vegetables, and potatoes. "Please, sit.

Anywhere you'd like. I'll get your iced tea. Or would you like something else with dinner?"

"I'll get it," Derek said, placing a hand on Jimmy's shoulder to stop him from moving to the living room. "Please, sit." He wondered what other surprises Jimmy had in store for him. He couldn't wait to find out everything about him.

"If you don't eat meat," Derek began as he settled himself at the table. "What will you be having for dinner?"

"Vegetables and potatoes," Jimmy explained. "And this," he said, pointing to a strange little colorless rectangular box on his own plate.

"What is that?" Derek saw the look on Jimmy's face and realized he must look as bewildered as he felt at that moment. "Sorry. Please forgive me. I didn't mean to be—"

"It's tofu," Jimmy explained. "Would you like to try some? It's really very good."

"Sure," Derek said, not sure if he would like it, but not wanting to insult him. He watched as Jimmy took a spoon, scooped up some of the tofu and passed the utensil. Derek took it, forced a smile, and prepared for the worst as he popped the colorless food into his mouth.

"Well?" Jimmy asked after a few moments.

"You know what?" Derek finished swallowing and raised his eyebrows. "It's not that bad."

Jimmy laughed, and Derek felt a wave of relief that he hadn't had to lie.

JIMMY TRIED not to look as Derek, his shirt riding up to expose his firm, hairy belly, leaned back in his chair.

"Man, I'm stuffed," Derek said, patting his exposed belly, then pulling his shirt back down. "Can't remember the last time I had a meal that good."

"Thank you," Jimmy said, tucking one foot under himself. "There's plenty left."

"No, no," Derek said, holding up his hand, palm toward the chicken. "If I eat anything else, I may just explode."

"But your dessert," Jimmy said, pointing a thumb behind him to the kitchen.

"I brought it more for you, to tell you the truth. I don't really have a sweet tooth."

"Well, what about Phil and Nick and... sorry, what was the other fella's name?"

"Clark," Derek said with a little chuckle, wondering how upset Clark would be if he found out Jimmy didn't even remember his name. "They'd never say no to food this good, even if it is leftovers."

"Okay, so I'll put four care packages together."

"Four?"

"In case you want some later," Jimmy said, raising himself out of his chair.

"Hang on," Derek said. "Please," he added when Jimmy turned to look at him. "I had another idea." He raised himself out of his chair and came around to Jimmy's side of the table. "I was hoping I could come by tomorrow and maybe we could have a picnic. Take Bozo and Miss Alicia. Maybe you know a nice place where we could sit in the shade and talk some more?"

"Miss Alicia's not too fond of the outdoors," Jimmy said. Derek thought he would hear a rebuff. "But Bozo and I love the outdoors."

Derek smiled and moved closer to Jimmy and placed his hand on one flushed cheek. He leaned in slowly and touched his lips to Jimmy's, his eyes closing instinctively. He heard his own moan as Jimmy caressed his chest and then settled his hand on his bicep. "It's a date, then," Derek whispered as he opened his eyes and took a step back.

"There's still plenty of food. Should I put something together for your bandmates?"

"I think they'd like that," Derek said and began to help Jimmy clear the table.

Chapter 7

JIMMY WAITED on the little deck that led from his upstairs apartment to the parking lot. Bozo was waiting beside him, and Jimmy absentmindedly stroked the pup's head and ears. Derek would be arriving any minute for their picnic. He'd instructed Jimmy not to prepare anything, that he would not need to lift a finger. Derek's exact words were difficult to remember. Well, any words that came after Derek referring to this picnic as their "second date" would be hard to remember.

As he sat on the top stair combing his fingers through his dog's silky fur, Jimmy had the usual argument with himself about getting involved with anyone. After his last relationship, Jimmy had sworn it would take an incredibly understanding and patient man to make him reconsider his recent vow of celibacy. And despite Derek's dismal first impression, or perhaps because of it, Jimmy found himself thinking that a long-distance flirtation might be a blessing in disguise. They would both get to know each other slowly, through letters, e-mails, and phone conversations. There would be time enough for Jimmy to figure out if Derek was as kind and patient as he wanted Jimmy to believe.

He heard a car drive over the gravel in the parking lot, heard the sound of a car door slam shut, and realized he was smiling. Derek appeared on the sidewalk, juggling several plastic bags. He didn't look up until Bozo started making his way down the stairs to offer his own greeting.

"Hey, Bozo. Hey, boy," Derek said, setting the bags on the grass so he could pick up his new friend. After a few seconds of nuzzling and sniffing, Bozo had his nose stuck into one of the plastic bags. "Yes," Derek said, looking up at Jimmy with a patient smile. "I brought you some more treats. And for Miss Alicia too."

"You didn't have to do that," Jimmy said as he slowly descended the stairs. "He still has your treats from last night."

"I know, but...." Derek shrugged his shoulders and waited for Jimmy to get closer. He put his arm around the shorter man's shoulder and placed a quick kiss on Jimmy's temple.

Jimmy inhaled deeply and wondered if Derek always smelled this good. "Let's get this stuff inside before Bozo eats it all." Jimmy kneeled down and scooped up the dog, tucking him under one arm while his free hand took two of the bags. Derek took the remaining two, and they headed up the stairs. Jimmy stopped on the deck and pointed to the south. "The river runs behind the bar, right over there, so I thought that would be a perfect place for our picnic."

"Sounds great," Derek said and followed him into the apartment.

"Miss Alicia might join us. She's okay for a little while, but she prefers the air conditioning." He put Bozo on the hardwood floor and then deposited his two bags on the counter. "And since we'll basically be in the backyard, it'll be easier to bring her back home if she doesn't like it."

Derek deposited his bags beside the others and then turned to look at Jimmy. "The boys say thanks for the leftovers. Phil wants to know if you'll marry him."

Jimmy laughed and moved to the hall closet to retrieve the wicker basket. "Well, it was my pleasure. And you let Phil know that I'll give it some thought." Jimmy put the basket on the counter, opened it to remove the plaid blanket, and offered a sly wink to Derek.

"I will most definitely tell him nothing of the kind," Derek said. He reached for Jimmy's hand, brought it to his lips, and kissed it softly. "I'm a good sport, but not an idiot."

"Fair enough," Jimmy said as they began to unload each of the four bags. "I made some chicken salad sandwiches on homemade buns for you—and the boys, if there are any left over."

"I'll make sure to leave some for them. I just brought some salads and dressing, some iced tea, and some containers of fruit salad for dessert." Derek reached into the last bag and pulled out a deli container.

"Oh, and I brought a few grilled veggie burgers for you." Derek held out the clear-plastic containers. "They have sprouts and arugula and some sort of dairy-free cheese."

"I know them well," Jimmy said, taking the containers and placing them inside the basket. "The owner of the deli, Mr. Sims, has a very rebellious daughter, a vegan. She's been twisting his arm to expand his menu. I was in there a couple of weeks ago to buy myself some potato salad as a treat, and he was telling me that he'd had to apologize to his wife because he didn't think there would be enough vegans around to make a profit." Jimmy stopped loading the basket and looked at Derek. "But from what he was saying, there are so many of us now that he's going to need to do some expanding of that particular section. Apparently, Mr. Sims does not like the taste of crow."

Derek laughed and began collecting the empty bags.

Jimmy placed a hand on his forearm to stop him. "Thank you for doing that." Jimmy looked back at the picnic basket and then focused on Derek's handsome face again. "That was very thoughtful." He leaned up and gave Derek a quick kiss. Then his nerves got the better of him, and he didn't try for a second, longer, kiss.

DEREK ACCEPTED the kiss and thought of wrapping his arms around Jimmy's trim waist and pressing his luck to quench some of his desire for this man. But he didn't. "It's the least I could do."

"Shall we get going?"

"Lead the way."

"If you wanna grab the basket, I think Bozo will follow you. So I'll just grab Miss Alicia and the blanket and lock up."

Derek took the basket off the counter and walked to the deck, smiling to himself as he watched Bozo follow him. He reared up and sniffed the basket whenever Derek stopped moving or slowed down.

"Okay, down the stairs and head to the back of the building," Jimmy instructed, Miss Alicia in his arms.

"She's not panicking or shredding your skin, so it's looking good," Derek said as he headed down the stairs, careful not to trip over the dog.

"This is one of the reasons I bought this place," Jimmy said as they made their way behind the building.

Derek took in the lush expanse of grass and the crystal clear river that couldn't have been more than fifty feet from the bar. There were coniferous and deciduous trees another twenty feet to the east, providing a natural privacy screen. Derek imagined that they would be a great shelter from strong winds during the winter months, as well. "Does the river freeze over in the winter?" He hadn't noticed that Jimmy had stopped at a little spot near the bank. He walked back a few feet and put the basket down, careful to keep an eye on Bozo.

"No, not really," Jimmy said, handing the blanket to Derek. "If you wouldn't mind spreading out the blanket? That way, I can put Miss Alicia right on the blanket."

"She *is* a lady, isn't she?"

"I know I spoil her, but it's nice to have her outside sometimes. I feel guilty when Bozo and I go for walks and she's all alone."

"That's not what I meant at all," Derek said, smoothing out the blanket and sitting cross-legged. "Here, I'll take her." With Miss Alicia in his lap, Derek heard the purring begin almost immediately. He watched as she took in her surroundings with no obvious signs of stress or anxiety. He was beginning to think that perhaps Jimmy was more bothered by Miss Alicia being outside than she was herself, but he refrained from saying anything.

Bozo was sitting protectively beside the basket, and Derek wondered just how intelligent this dog was. Jimmy was undoing straps and freeing plates and cups and utensils, placing them on the blanket. As Derek leaned back and watched his gentle, graceful movements, he was suddenly curious about what this man would be like on the dance floor.

"May I ask you a question?"

"Of course."

"A personal one?"

"Of course," Jimmy repeated and stopped his organizing to look at Derek.

"What kind of kid were you?"

"What kind?"

"Yeah," Derek said, offering a smile. "Were you the studious kind that never got in trouble, or were you one of those kids out back of the school trying to smoke a cigarette between classes?"

Jimmy looked down at his arrangement of plates, cups, and cutlery and shrugged. "Neither, I guess." He began to arrange the various foods in their containers. "I did well in school, and I've never smoked, so… I'm not sure what kind of kid I was."

Derek noticed that Jimmy's graceful movements had become somewhat less so. "I'm sorry, Jimmy, I, uh, I didn't mean anything by the question."

"I know." Jimmy leaned back on his heels and used his right hand to push the hair out of his eyes. "I'm sorry too. It's not a time filled with fond memories for me."

Derek heard the words and closed his eyes. *Fuck*, he thought, chastising himself. Having been a cop for so long, he had a pretty good idea what that usually meant. He reached over and rested his hand on Jimmy's knee. "Please, Jimmy. I'm sorry. Forgive me?"

"Of course," Jimmy said, patting Derek's hand. "It's not something I'm ashamed of. Not anymore anyway, and I *do* talk about my childhood sometimes, but not with… well…."

Derek didn't say anything. He knew all too well how to finish that sentence. Jimmy still saw him as a stranger. He'd allowed some physical contact and a kiss or two, so Derek knew Jimmy had obviously done some healing, either on his own or with a therapist. But Derek had no way of knowing how recently the scars had begun to heal. Had Jimmy had decades to work through the pain and confusion, or had it only been a few years? He had no option other than to trust Jimmy to let him know when he was ready for the next step. He watched as Jimmy busied himself with arranging food, filling cups, and putting out little morsels of human food for Bozo and Miss Alicia on their own little plates. He couldn't help but think that he'd messed things up.

"Well, I think everything's ready," Jimmy said after a few minutes of silence. "Dig in."

"This is wonderful," Derek said, forcing himself to overcome the awkwardness he'd created. He picked up his cup of iced tea and held it up. "Here's to warm sunny days, great food, beautiful scenery, and especially to new friends."

"Cheers," Jimmy said with a smile and touched his cup to Derek's. Then he reached across to take Miss Alicia off Derek's lap. "Okay, Bozo, Miss Alicia, these are your plates."

Derek inhaled deeply and let his shoulders relax and his apprehension melt away. He sipped his iced tea and then picked up his plate, eager to try Jimmy's chicken salad on homemade buns. He took a bite and closed his eyes. "This is better than my mother's."

"Thank you," Jimmy said, a flush creeping over his cheeks.

"How's your veggie burger?"

"Perfect, as usual," Jimmy said, extending his plate. "Try some. You can take a bite from the other end if you're squeamish about sharing."

Derek looked at Jimmy and narrowed his eyes. "Why would I be squeamish? I've already kissed you."

"True," Jimmy said and raised his eyebrows. "Try some. Go on. I'm always curious to see what carnivores think of veggie burgers."

"Challenge," Derek said as he took the plate. "Accepted." He picked up the burger and wondered if finding himself slightly aroused when taking a bite from the same side as Jimmy meant he was some sort of demented weirdo. He smiled and handed back the plate. He was trying to figure out how to spit it out gracefully when Jimmy began to laugh.

"Here," Jimmy said, offering a napkin. "I'm sorry for laughing, but you should see the look on your face."

Derek turned his head and tried to empty his mouth with as much grace as he could. "What do you mean, the look on my face? I was smiling!"

"Smiling? Is that what that was?" Jimmy took one of the plastic containers and held it open so Derek could deposit his napkin. "Kind of reminded me of a man going to the proctologist's office."

"That makes sense," Derek said with a sly grin after taking a few healthy mouthfuls of iced tea. "Considering that it tasted like something he might leave behind."

"Oh, come on! It's not that bad."

"You're right," Derek said, squinting as he studied Jimmy's handsome face. "So tell me. When, precisely, did your taste buds stop working?"

"I have excellent taste buds," Jimmy said as he took another bite of his veggie burger. "For example, when you kissed me, I could tell that you use Colgate toothpaste and prefer lattes."

"Wow," Derek said and picked up his own plate again. "Impressive. All I tasted when I kissed you was our future." Derek watched Jimmy's smile fade and immediately thought he'd stuck his foot in his mouth again. He watched, helpless, as Jimmy stood up. "Too much? I'm sorry." Jimmy moved to stand beside Derek. "It's just that when I'm with you—"

Jimmy crouched down and put a hand at the back of Derek's neck. They looked into each other's eyes, briefly, as their lips met. Derek closed his eyes, felt himself growing more and more aroused as Jimmy's tongue moved playfully over his lips. Then there was nothing. Derek opened his eyes and looked up just as Jimmy pushed against his chest. He obliged, lay back on the grass, and reached out with his hands to align their torsos. Within moments their lips were joined again while they caressed and explored with their hands.

Derek was working his hands underneath the waistband of Jimmy's jeans when the younger man pulled away. "Did I hurt you? Are you okay?"

Jimmy nodded and slid off to the side. "My turn to be sorry, I guess."

"What for?"

"I'm not usually this impulsive." Jimmy laughed and propped his head on his hand, his gaze focused on Derek. "I don't normally throw myself at men."

"That's the nicest thing anyone's ever said to me."

Chapter 8

JIMMY AWOKE before the alarm sounded, and his mind almost immediately turned to the five hours he'd spent with Derek the day before. As the muted light of early evening began to fade, they'd returned to the comfort of Jimmy's living room, the conversation becoming easier and more leisurely with each passing hour. Even after Jimmy had thrown himself at him, Derek had not made even the slightest attempt to take it any further. He was a perfect gentleman for the rest of the evening.

Before he left Derek had merely kissed Jimmy, briefly and with the slightest hint of tongue, and then held him close and caressed Jimmy's back and neck with his strong hands. Then, after offering some kisses and scratches to Bozo and Miss Alicia, Derek let Jimmy walk him to his SUV. He waved good-bye from the parking lot, his mind torn between gratitude and irritation. He was grateful for the return of his well-ordered and unruffled life but irritated that he had not allowed himself to take things further.

He played with Bozo's ears while Miss Alicia deposited herself on his chest, as usual.

"Don't get too comfortable, missy," Jimmy said as the cat slowly blinked at him. "Time for Bozo's walk soon. Isn't that right, Bozo?" Jimmy looked into his dog's eyes and smiled. He lay for another couple of minutes, thinking about how wonderful Derek had been with the two animals, and then sighed as he started to sit up slowly, sending Miss Alicia to the end of the bed.

He didn't bother showering right away, preferring instead to get dressed in a T-shirt and sweatpants. He called to Bozo as he exited the bedroom and headed to the kitchen to put a little bit of food in both of their bowls and refresh their water. Miss Alicia didn't complain, but Bozo looked absolutely crestfallen when he saw what little food there was.

"I have a surprise for both of you," Jimmy promised, lacing up his running shoes. "When we get back, you're both going to get some treats for being so well-behaved yesterday." Bozo's eyes widened, and Jimmy couldn't help but laugh out loud. "Sometimes I think you understand every word I say," he teased and waited for Bozo to drink his fill.

Jimmy put some plastic bags under the waistband of his sweats and then turned to find Bozo had assumed the position and was waiting patiently for his harness. With a quick good-bye to Miss Alicia, the two of them were off.

The morning air was cool, although that wouldn't last for much longer, and the grass held a few drops of moisture. It glistened and winked at Jimmy as he locked the door and then kneeled down to put the key into a little pocket in Bozo's harness. They descended the stairs quickly, and Jimmy wondered why Bozo was in a greater rush than other mornings. The dog was practically taking the stairs two at a time.

At the bottom of the stairs, Bozo suddenly stopped and began sniffing, focused intently on something near the mailbox. Mail delivery wasn't until one or two in the afternoon at the earliest, but Jimmy lifted the lid anyway.

How did I miss that on Friday? Jimmy pulled out a blue envelope. It was a very pretty color, the kind that probably had some fancy name like periwinkle or Bleu de France. He turned it over quickly to see the return address, but there was none, nor was there a stamp.

Furrowing his brow he opened the letter and scanned the single page, which was the same blue as the envelope. He saw Derek's name written in beautiful cursive at the bottom. Jimmy blushed as the smell of Derek's cologne finally made its way to his nostrils. Bozo barked once—or was it a whimper—and Jimmy looked down to see the dog with his front paws on his knee.

"Is this what you smelled?" Jimmy kneeled down and let Bozo sniff the letter and eventually lick the single page. "Okay, boy, let's go."

Jimmy didn't read the letter right away. He would do that when they were safe, away from the morning traffic. This area didn't get a lot, but with the winding road in front of the bar, he never let himself get distracted. He placated himself by bringing the letter to his nose every now and again, just so he could remember lying on top of Derek's solid body in the grass.

When he heard the usual honks, saw the usual smiling faces of the people who would wave at him and Bozo, he smiled and threw up his hand in recognition. He wondered if it showed on his face. Would these people he'd been waving to for so many years wonder why his smile was a little brighter? Would they turn to their passengers and ask, "Does he look different to you?"

Jimmy stopped a couple of times while Bozo sniffed the same spots he sniffed every morning, before deciding once again that they were not worthy of his deposits. And as usual, when they reached the abandoned junkyard with its rusty cars, trucks, and household appliances, Bozo pounced and spun around until Jimmy unclipped the lead from the harness. He never had to worry about Bozo running into traffic, since the junkyard was behind a ten-foot metal fence. The rusted and torn metal presented another problem, but after their first visit, Bozo had cut the pad on his front left paw and had never gone near that section of cars and appliances again. And Jimmy had trained him well enough that all he had to do was call, and Bozo would come running back.

Bozo preferred to run to the abandoned house and its forgotten flowerbeds. There was enough dirt still left in them—and Bozo had visited them enough to leave his own brand of fertilizer—that any future owner would have a spectacular garden in no time at all.

While Bozo went about finding the perfect spot, Jimmy pulled out the letter and began to read:

> *Today, (the best day of my life)*
>
> *Dear Jimmy:*
>
> *I honestly tried to remember today's date, but I'm unable to focus long enough. I could pretend it's because I'm old. I could even pretend that it's because of all the touring and the waking up in strange places. But I would be lying. The truth is that I was in complete control of my mental faculties until I met you. And it's the most amazing feeling!*

I know, in this day and age of e-mail and texting, that you were probably wondering what kind of crazy lunatic wants to write letters, and I know you might not understand right now. But trust me, you will. I want to know everything about you. I know it may take you some time, but I'm very good at being patient—especially when my impatience would mean I would have to try and forget you.

I wanted to thank you, for everything. For listening, for trusting me, for letting me in, even just a little. And I wanted to thank you for such an amazing dinner and an incredible afternoon. And thank you for the most perfect kiss I've ever had.

Derek, xo

DEREK PUT down his fork and looked at Phil. "Too cheesy?"

"No, not at all. You wrote what you were feeling. That's never cheesy," Phil said, wiping his mouth with a napkin. "I'm happy for you."

"You're sure?"

"That I'm happy for you? Yes."

Derek laughed and shook his head. "God, I feel like I'm thirteen again and trying to tell Shelly Mitchell that I want to hold her hand when I walk her home from school."

"Thirteen? Wow, late bloomer I guess."

"Shut up," Derek said as he watched the waitress deposit the check on the table. He took it and reached into his back pocket for his wallet. "Thanks for listening."

"Hey," Phil said, shrugging his shoulders. "I can put up with anything if there's a free breakfast." He finished his coffee and looked at Derek. "But if you don't mind my asking, what's with the sudden awkwardness? I mean, you've been in more men than a convention of proctologists."

"Maybe that's why," Derek said, knowing that Phil was perceptive enough to understand.

"Performance anxiety? Afraid you might not be able to when it counts?"

"Oh, no," Derek said, blushing to the tips of his ears. "I don't have any problems with that. I mean, just thinking about him is enough to—"

"Okay, I get the picture," Phil said, raising his hand. "So, then, what?"

Derek leaned back and toyed with the check, folding it into an airplane and then looking at his friend. "You know when we were first starting out, trying to find gigs, and we would play some place we thought would be a dive, and it turned out to be one of our best?"

"Sure."

"I think Jimmy's the one—the one who could change it all for me."

"So? What? You're afraid that he'll end up loving you back, and then you'll quit the band?"

"I don't know."

"Come off it, Diz. You're not fooling anyone, least of all me. You ask me, it looks like he's already changed it all for you."

Derek said nothing and picked up the check again before Phil could take it from him.

"You're not making any sense." Phil held up a couple of fingers. "First you're pursuing him like he's Cathy and you're Heathcliff. Then you write him a beautiful letter, explaining how you want to know everything about him. And now you're wondering if maybe he's gonna end up changing everything."

"But I've only known him for three days."

Phil leaned forward and winked. "Ain't love a bitch, huh? Come on. We got another four hours of driving ahead of us."

Derek got up and walked over to pay the cashier while Phil left the tip and headed to the parking lot. His mind was awash in opposing thoughts, the juxtaposition threatening to drive him absolutely crazy. *It's impossible to fall in love in three days. But if this isn't love, then what is it?* Derek had never felt this with any of his conquests. Or more precisely, he'd never felt this for anything longer than the time it took to get their clothes off.

Is that it? Derek headed out of the diner to join Phil. *Is that what this is? Once I sleep with Jimmy, this feeling will disappear, and he'll become just some other random name in a smartphone filled with fuck buddies?* The thought upset Derek, and the realization that he was angered by this thought made him even angrier. *What is going on?*

In the ten minutes it took Derek to drive himself and Phil back to the highway, he realized that his mind, even though inundated with incessant questions about Jimmy, kept coming back to only one: *How will I see Jimmy again while I'm on the road?*

Derek took it as a sign and wondered if Phil would be upset if they stopped again so he could call Jimmy.

Chapter 9

DEREK MANAGED to hold off on calling and let the anticipation build until he and Phil finally reached their hotel. Derek rushed to his room and had Jimmy's number dialed by the time he opened the door.

"Hello?"

"Hi, darlin'," Derek said, unable to contain his enthusiasm. He smacked his left knee when he remembered. "Sorry, I mean, Jimmy."

"You arrived safely?"

"That I did," Derek said, sitting down on the end of the bed. "I'm not interrupting anything, am I?"

"No, not at all. Ken and I are just setting up for the evening DFA." Jimmy laughed and Derek could hear another male voice in the background.

"The evening what?"

"DFA. As in 'do fuck all.' It's what Ken calls Mondays and Tuesdays."

Derek thought they were going to have bad cell reception from all the noise and the crackling on the line, but then everything disappeared, and he heard only the wonderful sound that was Jimmy's tenor.

"Okay, sorry. Had to get to a quieter place." Jimmy sighed and then the light, carefree tone returned. "Thank you for calling me. And thank you for the letter. It was beautiful."

Derek suddenly felt embarrassed. "My pleasure. Thank you for the wonderful weekend."

"I'd be lying to you if I told you that it wasn't one of the best days of my life as well."

"Yeah?"

"Yeah," Jimmy said with a whisper. "And I'd be an even bigger liar if I told you I'm not feeling the same things you are."

"Wow," Derek said, his lungs suddenly feeling as if there would never be enough air in them, ever again. His mind raced with all of the combinations and permutations that could be their life together. "Listen, I was hoping I could talk you into meeting me this coming weekend." There was nothing but silence on the other end of the phone, so Derek panicked. "I mean, if you want to, that is. Our next gig—I mean the band's next gig—will bring me three hours closer to you. We, I mean you and I, will only be three hours apart. So if you don't mind driving that long, we can meet Sunday morning and maybe spend some time together before—"

"Yes."

Derek closed his eyes and tried to will his heart from beating so fast. "Yes?"

"Yes."

"Okay," Derek said and couldn't help his giddy laughter. "Well, we're playing two different venues here, but then we'll be on the road to Collingsworth by Friday morning."

"Would you like me to come out for Saturday?"

"Fuck yeah," Derek said, his mind suddenly awash in the thought of spending several nights alone with Jimmy. "But what about the bar?"

"I think Ken can handle it. I've been thinking of making him the manager anyway."

"Two days," Derek said with a whisper. "Can't believe I'll get to spend that much time with you."

"Two days and one night."

Derek closed his eyes and imagined what it would be like—skin against skin, hands exploring, lips and tongues unable to get enough, to taste enough. He was sure he would never find anything more pleasurable, more erotic, than a night filled with Jimmy Campbell.

"Derek?"

"Sorry," Derek said, flushing a bright crimson, like he'd been caught with his father's Playboy magazines. "Can you bring Bozo and Miss Alicia?"

"I can't. Sorry," Jimmy said. "I've never taken them on a trip that long before, and Bozo isn't all that good with traveling, so...."

"Just the two of us, then," Derek said—a statement more than a question. "You're okay with leaving them with someone?"

"Of course. They've stayed with Sheila before. She has a Dachshund that thinks Miss Alicia is her long-lost sister. It's hilarious."

"Okay, well...." Derek searched frantically for another topic.

"Thank you again, for the letter."

"My pleasure, darlin'. Shit, sorry, I mean, Jimmy." Derek heard the chuckle on the other end of the line.

"I don't mind the darlin' so much now."

"Okay, then... darlin', would you mind if I call you again tonight, before you go to bed?"

"Well, that would actually be tomorrow morning. I don't usually get to bed before two or three in the morning."

"How about, say, ten or eleven tomorrow morning, then?"

"I'll be waiting."

"Okay then," Derek said, not wanting to end the conversation. "We'll talk soon."

"Yes, soon," Jimmy said, and Derek wasn't sure if he was actually detecting anticipation in the man's voice or if that was just wishful thinking. "Good night, Derek."

"Kiss Bozo and Miss Alicia for me?"

"I will."

"Sweet dreams, darlin'."

"Thank you. You too, Derek."

Derek forced his finger to punch the button and end the call. Exhausted and elated at the same time, he let himself fall back onto the bed. He was shaking his head at the realization that he was as nervous, as giddy, and as confused as he'd been when he was trying to figure out how to tell Shelly Mitchell he liked her. Of course hand-holding had been the objective when he was thirteen, and the year was 1976. But Jimmy wasn't Shelly Mitchell, and Derek knew a hell of a lot more about life than to settle for mere hand-holding. And that's why he was more nervous than a lawyer at the pearly gates.

He rushed out the door of his hotel room and banged on Phil's room.

Phil opened the door. "What?" He was standing in his underwear. Derek laughed and walked inside the room.

"Seriously? You answer the door in your underwear? What if I'd been a complete stranger?"

"I would have done a quick spin to lure you inside."

"Gross," Derek said, trying not to laugh. "So, he said yes. He's coming to meet me this weekend."

"Shall I alert the media?"

"Don't be a prick," Derek said, sitting on the bed that was still made.

"Relax, you big fairy. I'm happy for you." Phil returned to his bed and picked up his book. "Did you come for love-making tips?" he asked as he put on his reading glasses and smirked.

"Tips? Plural? Did you learn another one?"

"I don't know why I put up with you." Phil made a grand production out of sitting up and scratching himself before reaching for his socks and jeans.

"Because you're my best friend," Derek said sincerely. "I don't know what I would have done if you hadn't been there for me after the divorce."

"You're welcome," Phil said as he shrugged into a T-shirt. "Come on. We'll go get a drink, and you can tell me what's bugging you."

"KEN," JIMMY said as he walked behind the bar. "I have a proposition for you." Jimmy stood near the sink, his hip resting against the stainless steel edge. "I've been invited away for a couple of days this weekend, and I was hoping that you and Lori could handle things."

"Sure thing, Boss." Ken put down his clipboard, forgoing the inventory for a moment.

"I'll write out a routine, kind of a checklist if you'd like, so—"

"We can handle it, Jimmy. No need for a list. Lori and me, we know what needs doing."

"Fair enough."

"That was your proposition?" Ken picked up the clipboard.

"No, not exactly," Jimmy said as he reached for a dishtowel and headed to the sanitizer to empty the last of the glasses. "It looks like we may be losing Lori soon. I mean, she's been here since she finished high school. But, well, she started a foundation for LGBT youth not too long ago, and it seems to be picking up steam." Jimmy turned to look at Ken. "I mean, I've been donating, and I know she's been having great success getting other companies to donate. Anyway, I was thinking of maybe taking some more time for myself—"

"You're closing up? For good?"

"What? God, no!" Jimmy put the towel on the counter and moved closer to Ken. "Sorry. I'll get to the point. I was wondering if you'd like to try your hand at being the manager. You know, maybe see if it's something you'd be interested in."

"Manager?" Ken stopped his inventory and looked at his boss. "Seriously?"

Jimmy nodded.

"Well, yeah. I mean, if you think I can handle it."

"No doubt in my mind," Jimmy said, trying not to laugh at Ken's reaction. "Of course it would come with a substantial raise, and you'd need to help me replace you, do some interviewing and such. With me there, of course."

"Mindy's gonna flip out," Ken said, raking a hand through his long black hair. "I don't know what to say, Boss."

Jimmy extended his hand, and Ken shook it firmly. "Okay. So we'll start that today. So you should see a raise in your next paycheck. And of course we'll need to sign all of the necessary forms for the government... taxes, healthcare, and all that."

Ken nodded and reached into his pocket. "You mind if I call Mindy?"

"Sure," Jimmy said as Ken passed by and headed to the storeroom that Jimmy had exited five minutes before. *If only those beer kegs could talk.* A lot of intimate conversations had taken place in there over the years.

Jimmy reached for his own phone and laughed when he heard Ken's voice from down the hall. "Baby, you're not gonna believe this!"

He felt sorry for all of the other employers who'd dismissed Ken because of his criminal record. *Their loss is my gain.*

He dialed Sheila's cell phone to ask if she could take Bozo and Miss Alicia for the weekend—and was surprised when he heard her voice on the other end of the phone.

"Sheila? Hi. Sorry. I thought I'd get your voice mail."

"Okay, I'll hang up, and you can call back," Sheila said, her tone teasing, as always. "What's up?"

"I've been invited to visit with some friends in Collingsworth this weekend, just Saturday and Sunday, and I was hoping you could take care of Bozo and Miss Alicia."

"Of course," Sheila said, without hesitation. "But in all the years I've known you, I've never heard you mention any friends in Collingsworth."

"New friend," Jimmy said and regretted it. "Nothing serious, just a chance to get away."

"Jimmy?" He recognized that color in her voice and abandoned all hope of keeping Derek to himself. "Have you met someone?"

"His name is Derek," Jimmy said, certain he was blushing.

"And you were going to keep me in the dark?"

"Actually, I just met him this past Thursday, and to tell you the truth, I thought he was a complete creep."

"Oh. Okay. I forgive you, then."

"Thanks," Jimmy said, laughing.

"So, what changed your mind about him?"

"We had lunch on Saturday before he played here with his band. And then on Sunday, he came over for a picnic. He's so wonderful with Bozo and Miss Alicia, and they really seem to like him. And when he wants to be, he can be incredibly sweet and romantic, and...." Jimmy took a breath. "Sorry, I know I sound like an idiot, but I want to see where this goes."

"About fucking time," Sheila said after a moment. "I was beginning to think you were a robot. Like that 'Info' on that *Star Wars* program that Martin always watched on television."

"I think you mean 'Data,' and it was *Star Trek*."

"Whatever," Sheila sighed. "Okay, so you'll just leave them with me on Friday night, then?"

"Okay," Jimmy said, the feelings of guilt already working their way through his body like malignant creeping ivy. "Sounds good. I'll see you then."

The one consolation Jimmy clung to was that he would get to see Derek again, very soon—for two days and one night.

Chapter 10

DEREK SAT on the sofa, willing himself not to keep checking the window every few seconds to see if Jimmy had arrived. With every passing minute, his nerves were becoming more and more frayed. He'd tried rehearsing, but he kept forgetting the lyrics to the songs. He'd spent the previous hour exercising, doing sit-ups and push-ups in his hotel room but stopped when he realized that he would be too worn-out for the gig that night, not to mention what he had planned for him and Jimmy after that. So he sat on the sofa, his right leg bouncing at an ever-increasing speed until it felt numb from the friction of the denim against his skin.

He stretched out on the sofa, checked his cell phone one last time, and decided that he would try to meditate. He started slowly, breathing in through his nose and out through his mouth. He counted, trying to extend his count each time. It was working fine. His nervousness seemed to abate until his cell phone rang. He did an inelegant jackknife, his feet and long legs a jumbled turmoil as he lunged for his phone and nearly fell off the sofa.

"Hello?"

"Hi, Derek. It's Jimmy."

"Hey, darlin'. You here? You're in the parking lot?"

"Not quite. I just hit the city limits. I'm parked at a gas station. Another fifteen or twenty minutes and I should be at the hotel."

"Okay, take your time. Don't want you getting in an accident or anything. I'll be here."

"Are you okay?"

"Will be, soon as you get here."

"I'm serious. You sound worried, like you did before you asked me to come out for the weekend."

Derek thought about lying some more and telling Jimmy that he was okay, but he figured if he stood any chance with this man, he'd best be completely honest. It was one of the things Derek really liked about Jimmy—he knew a lot more about Derek than most people and was still willing to drive three hours to be with him. Derek wasn't looking to do anything to jeopardize that.

"Derek?"

"It's nothing, really, darlin'. I was, well, worried about you. You told me during the picnic that you like your life quiet, that you're not too fond of too many disruptions and such."

"You don't have to be worried about me. If I didn't want to be with you, I'd have said no."

"Okay. Thank you, Jimmy."

"You're welcome. Now, I have to hang up so I can get back on the road."

"Okay, I'll be waiting on you." *God, another thing to love about the man—he pulls over to talk on his cell phone.* Derek chastised himself for not doing the same more often.

JIMMY CLOSED his cell phone and tossed it into his backpack on the passenger seat. "Another twenty minutes," he said to the windshield as he turned the key and started his SUV. Jimmy would be nothing but a bundle of nerves until he was with Derek, until he could touch him and kiss him.

He'd spent the previous three hours debating with himself, vacillating on whether or not he should get it over with and rip the man's clothes off. Get the sex out of the way, first thing. But then another five miles down the highway, he'd be almost convinced that that would be a very bad idea. After almost three hours of arguing back and forth—and after hearing Derek's voice—he decided that he would leave that decision up to Derek. If he would be happy with some kissing and cuddling, like at the picnic, Jimmy wouldn't ask for more than what Derek wanted to take.

And then there was the other problem—when to tell Derek, how much to tell Derek, and of course, dealing with Derek's reaction. Would he shrug it off, as Alicia did all those years ago, and tell him he was stupid and to never do it again? Or would he suddenly become silent, distancing himself slowly, until Jimmy gave up trying to talk to him—as Jayson had?

Jimmy thought back to Jayson. Tall, educated, with soft red hair, Jayson was a high school gym teacher, a former athlete who'd chosen to dedicate his life to helping future generations. But Jayson had not been able to handle the news that Jimmy had once tried to kill himself. Whatever Jayson's reason, he'd kept it to himself. Jimmy turned his SUV onto Somerset Street and headed west to the hotel. *Funny, isn't it? That was seventeen years ago that Jayson disappeared from my life, and I've never bothered to try and figure out why.*

He'd always figured the reason was a phrase he'd come to associate with Alicia—"Dirty hands, pure heart. Pure hands, dirty heart." Jimmy had heard her say it several times before he finally asked her to explain it. It was the title of a story she'd written about a princess who was locked away in a castle by an evil wizard. She thought she would be saved by the white knight, his heart aching and pining for her, only to discover that he'd been able to forget her rather quickly. Her savior was actually the dirty, grimy young man who was covered in pig shit because he worked on his father's farm. Alicia had summed it up in only a couple of sentences. "Sometimes, they'll tell you they want to help you, but then when they see the long, dirty road they'll need to travel to get to you, it turns out they don't really want to get dirty. The ones who'll run or walk or crawl to get to you? Those are the ones you wait for."

Jimmy smiled as he remembered Alicia, as he remembered how much fun it had been to sit with her in the garden of the hospital, listening to her stories, her advice, her promises to come and see him when she was in remission. His smile faded, and he looked up when he heard the honking. The light was green. He accelerated through the intersection and saw the sign for the hotel up ahead.

By the time he was safely parked, the smile was back on his face. Thinking about Alicia and how much he missed her made him think about the gentle cat who was her namesake, and her canine shadow. He shook his head, chastising himself for becoming so nostalgic, and removed the key from the ignition. As he turned to open the door, he jumped in his seat.

"Sorry!"

Jimmy laughed and opened his door. "It's okay. You just startled me," Jimmy said as he walked toward Derek and looked around quickly. "What are your thoughts on public displays of affection?"

"I'm game," Derek said, wrapping his arms around Jimmy and kissing his temple. "God, you smell so good."

Jimmy closed his eyes and pressed his nose against Derek's strong shoulder. *God help me.* He inhaled the crisp smell of a fresh cotton shirt and the cologne that instantly brought back memories of the picnic.

"God," Derek whispered in his ear. "I missed you."

"Me too," Jimmy said, feeling feeble. He felt one more kiss to his temple, and then Derek was pulling away.

"Let me get your luggage."

"Thank you," Jimmy said as Derek opened the back door. He reached to the passenger side and grabbed his backpack, then pressed the button to lock all the doors.

"Okay," Derek said, hoisting the little carry-on and ignoring the roller wheels. "Just this little one?"

"Just the one," Jimmy said, with a smirk. "It's only for two days."

"And one night." Derek lagged behind long enough to pat Jimmy's ass. "Are you hungry?"

"Not really," Jimmy said as they headed through the front door and toward the bank of elevators. "But if you want to eat, I guess I could eat something light."

"Actually, I'm not really hungry. I thought we might just stay in the room and watch a movie or something. Unless you want to take a nap after the long drive?" The elevator arrived, and the two men shuffled inside. "I got extra towels in case you wanted to take a shower or something."

The doors closed, and Jimmy leaned up and kissed Derek on the lips—a tender, chaste kiss. "You're very thoughtful," he said before stealing one more. "I wouldn't mind taking a shower. When's your show tonight?"

Derek checked his watch. "Not until ten tonight."

"So that gives us, what, eight hours to kill? Of course you'll probably need to get there early to do all your setting up and sound checks, huh?"

"Yeah, but eight hours sounds about right."

The elevator arrived at the fifth floor, and Derek led the way to the room. Jimmy lagged behind a little, wondering how—or even if—he should tell Derek about the scars. He knew himself well enough to know that he wouldn't be able to resist Derek's charms much longer. He wanted this man. He wanted to run his fingers through his chest hair, wanted to taste and lick every inch of him. He wanted to look up and see Derek's hooded blue eyes looking down at him, the two of them mesmerized—moaning and grunting as Derek pumped into him over and over. But before that, Jimmy had to find the guts to tell Derek about the scars he would eventually find.

"So," Derek said, placing the suitcase on the unused queen-size bed. "Did you want to clean up first, or maybe you'd like to take a nap, or maybe I—"

Jimmy pressed himself against Derek's solid chest, placed his hands at the back of his neck, and brought their lips together. He closed his eyes as Derek's big hands wrapped around his torso. Their bodies aligned perfectly—hips pressing against hips, erections straining against clothing and body heat. Derek moved his hands up and down, again and again, always stopping at the waistband of Jimmy's jeans.

Without allowing so much as a millimeter between their bodies or lips, Jimmy felt bold enough to take some initiative. He reached behind him, took one of Derek's hands, and pushed it, not so gently, under the waistband of his own jeans. It was a silent invitation for Derek to explore fully. And when Derek let go a guttural sound that Jimmy felt career straight to his own groin, he began pulling and pawing at Derek's clothes.

"Wait," Derek said. "I made plans for our first time."

Jimmy pulled back to look at Derek. "Plans?" Jimmy felt the hazy fog lift slightly, and he finally understood what Derek was saying.

"Yeah," Derek admitted. "Want to take my time. Spend hours learning what makes you moan and where you're ticklish and—"

Jimmy leaned up and kissed Derek again, his hands resting on his shoulders. The urgency was gone, the kiss chaste. After they ended the kiss, Jimmy rested his forehead on Derek's muscular, hairy chest. "Sorry, I wasn't thinking."

"'S okay, darlin'," Derek said, his tone playful once again. "Can't really believe it, myself. Me stopping you just now. But, well, you deserve better than a quick fuck. For the first time, anyway."

Jimmy laughed as he saw the flush creep up Derek's face. "I cannot believe that this is the same guy who threw all those lines at me a week ago."

"Ten days, actually," Derek said, tucking his shirt back in.

They stared at each other for a few moments before Jimmy finally spoke. "Well, I'll go get cleaned up."

"In a minute," Derek said, wrapping his arms around Jimmy's waist. "Have I thanked you yet for being here?"

"In a manner of speaking," Jimmy said, letting his hands travel down to rest on Derek's ass. "Have I thanked you yet, for inviting me?"

By way of an answer, Derek brought their lips together for a brief kiss before releasing Jimmy and turning him toward the bathroom.

Chapter 11

JIMMY SAT at the bar with a beer in one hand while the other picked nervously at the edge of a coaster shaped like a big rig's wheel. The expansive room was divided by a conspicuous trophy case into one section with tables and another for dancing. The trophy case was predominantly glass and was filled to bursting with awards and memorabilia highlighting the patrons' expertise in rodeo and shuffleboard.

The place seemed like it hadn't had a good cleaning in a very long time. Jimmy liked the scarred, ancient tables set against the dull concrete floor that led to gleaming hardwood as the bar area gave way to the dance floor on the other side of the trophies. As was his habit, Jimmy couldn't help imagining what he would do with the place if it were his bar.

The petite blonde behind the bar deposited another bottle in front of him. Jimmy looked at her. "From Derek," she said, offering a knowing smile.

"Thank you," Jimmy said.

"He gave me very specific instructions," she explained, going back to drying a tray of beer mugs. "Told me to make sure you always have a smile on your face and a beer in your hand."

Jimmy nodded and blushed, thankful that she looked away. He drained his first beer before placing this most recent one on the coaster. He looked toward the back of the bar, where Derek and Phil had disappeared.

"Derek tells me you own your own bar in Wainwright?"

"Just outside of, yes." Jimmy took a sip of his beer. "It's nothing quite like this, though."

"Well, thank you," the barkeep said, extending her hand. "Julie."

"Jimmy."

"Nice to meet ya, Jimmy."

"Likewise, Julie. Are you the owner?"

Julie nodded, picked up the towel, and draped it over her shoulder. "Going on ten years now."

"Congratulations," Jimmy said, feeling himself relax.

"I should say the same to you," Julie said, offering a lopsided smile and a wink. "Derek's real sweet on you."

"The feeling's mutual," Jimmy said as the heat traveled to the tips of his ears.

"Been telling that idiot for the past ten years he needs to find a beautiful man of his own and settle down."

"Ten years?"

"Yeah," Julie sighed. "I've known Derek for almost twenty. We used to work on the force together before I got shot one night. Derek had already left the force by then, and Beth, but he still made sure that my wife was looked after until I got out of the hospital."

"I'm so sorry."

"Me too," she said with a resigned smile. "Left the force once I got out of the hospital. Couldn't stand watching what the worry was doing to Suzie."

Jimmy assumed that Suzie was the wife. He thought of Derek—tall, handsome, and proud in his uniform. He wondered what it would have been like, sitting home, night after night, worried about whether or not he would make it home in one piece. "Suzie sounds like a very strong woman."

"That she is," Julie said, her face immediately transformed by a big smile. "Anyway, if it hadn't been for Derek and the boys playing here for free for the first year, I don't think we'd be doing so well now."

"Do you run this place together?"

Julie nodded. "Once we got busy enough, Suzie gave up her job as a music teacher, and we've been running this place ever since."

"That's great," Jimmy said. "Nothing quite like making your dreams come true, huh?"

"No, sir," Julie said, her eyes moving to the front door as it opened. "Speak of the devil."

Jimmy turned to see a tall brunette stride into the bar.

"Suzie? This here is Jimmy."

Jimmy stood and offered his hand. "Suzie, it's so nice to meet you."

"She been telling you our life story, I see." Suzie's smile belied any real annoyance.

"This is Derek's Jimmy," Julie said, raising her eyebrows.

"*That* Jimmy," Suzie said, placing a hand on his shoulder. "Well, this is a real honor. Never thought I'd meet a man who could make that man think with anything other than his—"

"Suzie!"

"It's okay," Jimmy said, laughing as he motioned to the seat next to his. "Please." Suzie sat. "It wasn't a very good start, I'm afraid."

"He try all that 'around you, I'm just Dizzy' shit?"

Jimmy laughed and nodded.

"Can't believe that crap actually works on grown men."

"He's really very charming," Jimmy said, suddenly feeling protective of Derek.

"Charming and generous and attentive and one of the nicest men we know," Julie said after a moment. "But for some reason, I guess he felt the need to stretch that phase out for almost ten years. Fucking every little twink who looked at him." Julie's expression turned to one of shame, or perhaps guilt. "Sorry. Forgive me."

"It's okay," Jimmy said, taking another sip from his beer. "Derek's been very honest with me. As I have been with him." A sense of guilt washed over Jimmy as he remembered that he had yet to explain what Derek would find on his inner thighs.

"Well, I for one am very happy for both of you," Suzie said, placing her hand on Jimmy's forearm. "Okay. I'm heading back to the office to work on the books." Looking at Jimmy, Suzie added, "Save me a dance?"

"Sure thing."

Jimmy and Julie both said their good-byes, and Suzie headed to the back of the bar.

DEREK AND the other members of the band were just heading out of the back room to do their sound check when he noticed Suzie approaching.

"Hey, Suzie!" Derek said, opening his arms wide for a hug.

"Hey yourself," she said, walking into his arms and wrapping her own tightly around his waist. "Met Jimmy," she whispered against his neck. "You do anything to fuck that up and I'll kick your ass."

Derek laughed and gave her one quick squeeze before releasing his friend. "No chance of that," he said, placing a quick kiss on her temple.

"Good," she said before greeting the other band members.

The five of them exchanged pleasantries for a moment before Suzie continued to the office. Derek was smiling, thinking of how Jimmy must have worked his charms on Suzie and Julie. *No. No chance of me letting that man go.*

Derek made it to the stage, followed closely by Clark, Phil, and Nick. Derek took his seat at the keyboard, looked out at the bar, and found Jimmy staring at him and smiling. He offered a quick wink and began the sound check, his mind going in too many different directions at once. While trying to focus on the first song, he was thinking about what he would be doing later that evening, naked and alone with the sexiest man he'd met in a very long time.

Julie gave him the thumbs-up after a few bars. There was no in-house engineer, so it was a matter of checking all of the mics that would be open during the performance and extrapolating for the fact that the bar would be filled with people and not empty as it was at that moment. After ten years Derek and Phil were more than experienced enough to know the levels that would optimize the music and vocals. And having played this particular bar four or five nights a week for more than a year, Derek knew by rote what those levels were.

"This next song," Derek whispered into the mic. "Is dedicated to that fine-looking man sitting at the bar." He smiled as Jimmy shook his head, looking embarrassed. Derek began to sing "All That Heaven Will Allow" by the Mavericks and stopped after the first chorus. Another thumbs-up from Julie.

After checking the mics for Phil and Clark, Derek got up and headed to sit beside Jimmy.

"Thank you," Jimmy said, his voice low and seductive. "That's one of my favorite songs."

"My pleasure, darlin'."

"And thank you for having Julie take care of me."

"And you met Suzie, I heard."

"They've both been lovely to me." Jimmy leaned over and kissed Derek on the cheek. "That was a wonderful thing you did for them."

Derek's brow furrowed for a moment. "Ah, I see they've been telling stories about me."

Jimmy leaned over once more, and Derek obliged him with a kiss on the lips. They kissed gently for a few seconds, and then Derek let his head rest against Jimmy's neck.

"I wish it was later," Derek said, placing a quick, final kiss by Jimmy's ear.

"Only a few more hours," Jimmy said, caressing the strong thigh pressing against his own. "Trust me. I'll make it worth the wait."

Derek growled, sat back up, and looked at Jimmy with heavily lidded eyes. "The things I'm gonna do to you." With one last look in Jimmy's eyes, he pushed himself away from the bar.

THE BAND was a huge success. The crowd yelled requests throughout the two-hour performance, and Derek and the boys tried their best to accommodate each one. Jimmy danced most of the evening away—with a few men who'd asked him, with Suzie a couple of times, and even with Julie while the band played their cover of "Something Stupid." He hadn't done a slow dance in more years than he could remember, but once he let Julie lead—both of them laughed at Jimmy's fumbled attempts—he enjoyed himself for the first time in a very long while. The bar was not his worry this evening, so he had nothing to do but enjoy himself.

By midnight, there was nothing left for Jimmy and Derek but what each of them had been craving for too many days to count. But Jimmy had still not figured out how to explain the scars on his inner thighs. He waited outside the bar, the back of his shirt sticking to his sweat-soaked skin.

"Okay, darlin'." Derek was walking toward Jimmy. "I think the first thing we should do is have a shower."

"Derek?" Jimmy leaned against his solid chest, intent on telling the truth and letting the cards fall where they may.

"Yeah, darlin'?" Derek moved his hand to rest on Jimmy's back. "Geez, you're soaking wet."

"I know. I haven't danced that much in years."

"Well," Derek said, placing both of his hands on Jimmy's back. "I should warn you that I can get pretty sweaty too." He pulled their bodies together, and Jimmy felt the exquisite sensation of Derek's impressive erection against his belly. "I want you," Derek whispered against Jimmy's lips. "God, I want to lick every inch of this body, want to be inside you. I never wanted anyone so much."

Jimmy's resolve crumbled. He'd imagined he would be strong enough to tell Derek about the scars, about what he'd been through. But he just couldn't. He was too frightened by the possibility that things would change. And even more frightened by the possibility that he would be driving back home within the hour because he'd taken the easy way out. He felt like a coward, but pushed those feelings down deep. *Maybe Derek wouldn't notice them?*

"Derek, please," Jimmy sighed as Derek traced a path to his ear with his lips. "I need you."

"All yours, baby." Derek took Jimmy's hand and led him to the car. "For as long as you want." Derek opened his door and then walked around to get in the driver's seat.

Jimmy was in no condition to drive. Not only had he had a total of four beers, his arousal was so thick that there was no way Jimmy could have navigated the unfamiliar streets. Derek, on the other hand, had not had one drink, and his own arousal seemed to make him even more focused on arriving safely at the hotel.

When they got on the hotel elevator, Jimmy looked up at Derek. They were mere seconds from arriving at their floor.

"Just so you're not surprised—once we're through the door, I'll be taking off your clothes and mine, and then we'll be in the shower, where I plan to make you come harder than you've ever done before."

The bell sounded, the doors opened, and the two of them practically sprinted to the room. Once inside Jimmy quickly undid the buttons of Derek's shirt, then pressed him up against the wall and sank to his knees. He deftly popped the button on the big man's jeans and reached inside to free his straining erection.

"Sorry to spoil your plans, but I've wanted to do this ever since the picnic," Jimmy said. Then he nipped and massaged Derek's foreskin. Their moans mingled, Derek's punctuated with hisses and encouragement as Jimmy swallowed the entire length of his engorged cock.

"Jesus, darlin'," Derek said, his hands resting gently on the top of Jimmy's head. "Fuck, yeah. Take the whole thing."

Jimmy did as he was told and took the entire length into his mouth. The smell of Derek's musk and sweat made him dizzy with desire. He pulled off for a moment. "Tell me what you like."

"Rub your hands up and down my belly and chest."

Jimmy followed the instructions, his own erection straining against his jeans.

"Yeah, fuck," Derek muttered.

Jimmy looked up as he tongued the slit to see that beautiful hairy chest heaving up and down. "Look at me," Jimmy said. When he saw Derek's eyes, he swallowed the entire length again and pressed his forehead against the flat belly.

"Oh, stop. Please," Derek grunted as his hands pushed against Jimmy's head. "Please, don't wanna come yet."

Jimmy pulled back and watched as Derek sank down to the ground and removed his shirt. Derek's hands made short work of Jimmy's shirt and jeans.

"Fuck me," Derek said as he saw Jimmy wasn't wearing any underwear. "Feel like I'm about to explode."

Derek kissed and sucked and used his tongue on just about every inch of the toned body in front of him. Jimmy sighed as he felt his own cock wrapped in the wet heat of Derek's mouth. He ran his fingers through the thick head of salt-and-pepper hair and massaged the scalp, his movements mirroring the slow, methodical up-and-down motion of Derek's head. "Please, Derek, so close. Don't wanna come yet," Jimmy echoed as he pulled Derek up by the shoulders.

Derek caressed and massaged anything he could reach while he brought his lips down on Jimmy's. Their tongues met, and Jimmy thought he would come just from the thought that they were tasting each other and themselves at the same time. Derek hooked one of Jimmy's legs with his elbow and lifted it so that he could tease Jimmy's entrance with his engorged cock.

"What do you want, darlin'?"

"Fuck me," Jimmy panted. "Condoms in my jeans."

"Already there," Derek said as he let go of Jimmy's leg and reached down to his ankles to pull a condom out of his back pocket. "Shit, lube."

"Just use spit. I don't care."

"Hang on," Derek said as he pushed himself off the floor. He quickly disentangled his legs from his jeans and boxers and moved to the nightstand between the two beds. "You've got me all turned around, baby." Derek found the container of lube and returned to stand over Jimmy.

"Jesus, Derek. You have an incredible body." Jimmy looked him up and down—long, muscular legs, slim hips, heavy, uncut cock, and a torso that defied description. He had a taut belly with a scattering of salt-and-pepper hair that became thicker as it covered his perfectly formed pecs.

"And it's all yours," Derek said as he lowered himself to his knees. He ripped open the package with his teeth, put on the condom, and slicked himself. "Come here, darlin'," Derek said, hooking his arms under Jimmy's knees and lifting until his hole was right in front of Derek's face. "Gonna get you ready for me."

"Yes," Jimmy panted. He closed his eyes as he felt the hot tongue poking and probing for what seemed like hours.

"Open up for me, baby," Derek said, his torso hovering over Jimmy. "Wanna make you feel good."

Jimmy's legs were still in the crook of Derek's elbows, so he relaxed as much as he could before he felt the exquisite pain of that beautiful cock pushing inside.

Chapter 12

JIMMY PUSHED Derek up against the back wall of the shower and stroked him with his hand while their tongues pushed against each other. Derek couldn't remember the last time he'd been able to come this many times in one night. He had no idea what time it was and he didn't really care. If this gorgeous man wanted to stay up all night, Derek was more than happy to oblige.

"I'm sorry," Jimmy said as he rested his forehead against Derek's. "I know I should leave you alone, and we should probably get some sleep."

"I'm not complaining," Derek said as he stroked Jimmy's erection.

"I feel like a man who's been lost in the desert for too many years."

"Come here," Derek said, turning him around. He pressed his erection against Jimmy's back as his hands caressed his chest and abs. "Beautiful body."

"How much time do we have before the water turns cold?" Jimmy turned himself to face Derek and found that thick, uncut cock with his hand.

"Anytime, I guess," Derek said, and he stuck his tongue inside Jimmy's ear. "Wanna finish this in bed?"

Jimmy reached past Derek's rock-hard ass, turned off the water, and reached for a towel.

"Forget about drying off," Derek said as he led Jimmy out of the shower, a towel in his hand. "Come here," he said as he got on the bed on his knees and placed the towel in front of him. Jimmy climbed up on his knees, facing him, and Derek placed one hand behind Jimmy's neck and used the other to pull on his cock. Jimmy did the same.

Derek lost himself in the sensation overload. They licked tongues while they brought each other to yet another climax. Derek thrust his hips several times into Jimmy's tight grip, and when Jimmy began to tongue one of his ears, Derek cried out and lowered his head to Jimmy's shoulder.

"Fuck," he muttered as he swiped his thumb over Jimmy's slit until Jimmy cried out his name. Derek was sure he'd never heard a more incredible sound than his name coming from those swollen lips. They rode out their orgasms. Derek didn't let go of Jimmy until they both collapsed on the bed. "Jesus Christ," he whispered as Jimmy snuggled against his side.

Neither spoke for a few minutes, each content to lie with their arms around each other.

"Have I thanked you for being here yet?"

Jimmy laughed, pulled himself closer to Derek, and combed through his thick chest hair. "My pleasure, darlin'."

"That's my line," Derek said, placing a hand over Jimmy's as it caressed his chest.

"You really do have a spectacular body," Jimmy said, placing lazy kisses on Derek's shoulder and neck. "It's hypnotic watching all of the muscles flex while you're pumping inside me." Jimmy raised his head and looked down at Derek's naval. "And the way this tattoo moves as you're belly muscles ripple when you come."

"Keep talking like that and we're not going to get any sleep at all."

"Does it mean anything?"

"No, just a dream catcher."

"It's beautiful work."

"Thank you."

Derek closed his eyes and wondered if he should ask Jimmy about the scars he'd noticed on the inside of his thighs. He'd wanted to stop and ask, but he was too much of a pig to stop himself. Besides, he rationalized, if there were anything for him to know, Jimmy would have said something, or would say something eventually. For the moment Derek was more than content to lie there with Jimmy caressing his chest and belly and let the entire evening sink in. *He's here with me. He came all this way because he wanted me. Probably not as much as I wanted him, but I'll take whatever this man wants to give me.*

"I really enjoyed meeting Julie and Suzie. And seeing Phil and Nick again was nice. I don't think Clark has forgiven me yet."

"Don't worry about Clark. He's young—just like we all were at one time." Derek disentangled himself and sat up. "Come on. Let's go to bed." Derek led Jimmy to the other bed, and they both settled under the sheets. Once they were settled and Jimmy laid his head on his chest, Derek continued. "Julie and Suzie were two of a very small group of people who didn't turn their backs on me when I left the force and came out."

"They're very grateful to you for what you did."

"We're kinda like family in a way," Derek said, and placed a kiss on the top of Jimmy's head. "And now you are too, if you want."

"Sounds good to me. Thank you."

Thinking about that one word, *family*, Derek pulled Jimmy closer. He wrapped both arms around Jimmy and kissed him once on the forehead. "Sweet dreams, darlin'."

"Good night, Derek."

JIMMY WOKE and immediately thought about getting the food out for Bozo and Miss Alicia. He would need to take Bozo out for a walk. He sat up and felt momentarily confused by his surroundings. Then he remembered where he was and with whom. He smiled to himself and looked down on Derek's handsome face, which was made even more attractive by the look of contentment that softened his rugged features. Unable to control himself, he rolled over and practically smothered Derek with his lips and body. But Derek didn't complain.

An hour later Jimmy wiped the sweat from Derek's forehead and let his hands rest on his strong shoulders, then pulled Derek so he was resting on top. Their breathing was labored, and both of their bodies were sensitive and exhausted from making love. Derek combed his hands through Jimmy's hair and kissed whatever skin he could reach. Jimmy just held onto Derek and recovered from their powerful release.

"Am I too heavy?" Derek whispered in his ear. He pulled out and reached down for the condom.

"Don't move," Jimmy said, his lips finding Derek's ear. "Don't move."

"Just need to...." Derek brought his knees up to rest beside Jimmy's hips and then braced his hands on either side of his solid shoulders. "Not so hard on my knees this way."

Jimmy laughed and pulled Derek's head down for a slow, soft kiss. "Sucks getting older, huh?"

"That's not the part that sucks," Derek said, smiling and taking another kiss. "It's not being where I thought I would be by this age."

"Where did you think you'd be by now?"

"You know," Derek sighed, letting his body come to rest on Jimmy's so that they were chest to chest. Derek's head was resting on Jimmy's shoulder, his warm breath caressing his neck. "I thought I'd have my shit together by now. Not fighting with an ex-wife over spoiled kids and their overdeveloped sense of entitlement."

"How is your shit not together?" Jimmy wrapped his arms around his muscled shoulders and caressed his wide back. "You're doing what you love to do. You make sure your family has everything they need. You've surrounded yourself with good friends like Julie and Suzie, and of course, your bandmates."

"I just wish I'd been more courageous and come out when I was younger, ignored all of the crap I let myself believe about fags being sick and depraved pedophiles." Derek moved his body so he was lying next to Jimmy, their bodies still making almost constant contact. "I just think about all the wasted time, how it could have all been so different if I hadn't been so selfish."

Jimmy reached down, pulled the condom off Derek's impressive cock, and reached for a tissue. He wrapped it in the tissue and tossed it on the nightstand. "Selfish?" Jimmy looked at Derek and saw the residual pain in his eyes. "What you did was *not* selfish." He turned on his side, pushed Derek onto his back, and let his hands rest in his thick, salt-and-pepper chest hair. "You didn't think you were gay, but you did think that you loved Beth. Where's the selfishness in that?"

"I think I knew that I wasn't really in love with Beth—"

"So?" Jimmy carded his fingers through Derek's chest hair, losing themselves in the intimate feeling. "We can only make the best decision based on all of the information we have at the time. I've made plenty of mistakes thinking that something was my fault when it wasn't."

Derek didn't say anything in return, just squeezed him a little more. Jimmy realized that this was probably the most appropriate moment to finally confess to Derek.

"The scars on my thighs are from years of cutting myself because I thought that not trying to stop my father from doing... things... to me meant I really wanted it to happen. It's what he told me all the time. And he managed to convince me that it was all my fault."

"I'm sorry, darlin'." Derek kissed his temple. "You were wrong to think that."

"And that's what I'm saying to you right now. Do you honestly think that *thinking* you might be gay means you are? I'm sure there are many men who might think that, because they have a crush on another boy or another man or because they have one experience and enjoy it." Jimmy kissed Derek's chest and then leaned up for a kiss on his lips. "Perhaps it just means that those men are very open to their feelings for a fellow human being. I mean, you obviously had sex with Beth, and I'm assuming you enjoyed it, even if only sometimes, right?"

Derek nodded.

"So, could that be because you're a very sensitive man and that you care about other people? That you can find sexual pleasure with either men or women, depending on your feelings for them?"

"You mean bisexual?"

"Not necessarily," Jimmy said, wondering how he could get his point across. "If you're looking for sexual pleasure, it seems that you've gravitated to men over the last few years, since your divorce."

Derek nodded again.

"Did you find each of those encounters pleasurable?"

"No, not really. But I did come each time."

"That's just biology," Jimmy said with a little chuckle. "And each time you did come, was it with the same trembling arms and legs like yesterday and today? Or did some of those experiences pale in comparison?"

"Darlin', everyone pales in comparison to you."

"I'll take that as a *yes*. And quit trying to charm your way out of this."

"Okay. I see what you're saying." Derek kissed the top of his head. "What about you? Have you ever had sex with a woman?"

"No. But I'm sure there's a woman out there somewhere who I could have an emotional connection with, and maybe that would be enough for me to try."

"So, you think you might be bisexual?"

"No. But I don't believe in labels like that. I think there are people who are just so sexual that they can get off with a man or a woman. But people like me, I need a deeper connection. There needs to be something that I find so incredibly irresistible about the person before I can imagine doing anything with him or her."

"So, you're an emotional bisexual." Derek winked when Jimmy looked up at him.

"Yes, you smartass," he said, pulling on Derek's chest hair. "I'm an *emotional* bisexual." He grabbed Derek's hand and kissed it. "Although, I think emotional bisexuals are probably better described as 'human.'"

"I get it," Derek said. He kissed Jimmy sweetly on the lips. "Thank you for telling me about your scars. I can't imagine how difficult that time must have been for you."

"Just part of my past, that's all." Jimmy raised a hand and stroked Derek's cheek, his thumb coming to rest on his bottom lip. "I ended up in the hospital. I met a wonderful girl named Alicia who helped me see things the right way. And my dad disappeared from my life."

"That's a very good attitude to have."

"And it's a lie," Jimmy said, glancing up at Derek's face. "I was really nervous about how I was going to tell you and what your reaction might be."

"My reaction?"

"There was one man, in the past, who—I don't know—maybe thought I was unstable or would flip out on him or something. It wasn't pretty." Jimmy looked at Derek, relieved that the man didn't seem bothered by his past. "I was going to tell you out in the parking lot, before we came back to the hotel, but I chickened out. I was afraid you wouldn't want damaged goods."

"Ah, darlin'," Derek said as he kissed Jimmy's temple. "We're all damaged in some way. Makes me angry to think a father could do that to his own kid, and even angrier that you thought any of it was your fault, but that other guy is an idiot. You seem pretty stable to me," Derek said, caressing Jimmy's shoulder. "Besides, it's not your problem if that flake couldn't see past the scars."

"Maybe," Jimmy said, snuggling closer. "Sometimes, it seems like a lifetime ago, but then something will happen and I'll remember how lost and confused I was, and it's like I'm still trapped there, in that hospital."

"Well, I'm no Miss Alicia, but think of yourself trapped there with me from now on."

"No," Jimmy said, caressing Derek's chest. "Can't imagine feeling that way now that you know the truth."

"And how do you feel right now?"

"Relieved and happy that you understand."

"I do, baby." Derek kissed his temple. "I'd be lying if I said there weren't a few moments when I thought about ending it all, especially just after the divorce. But I had my music to hold on to. And now, you have me."

Derek rolled onto his back, coaxing Jimmy's head to rest on his chest. He took a deep breath and let it out slowly.

"Isn't it strange what we put ourselves through?" Derek asked as he stroked Jimmy's back. "What we tell ourselves in order to try and find some peace? We put ourselves through hell thinking that heaven is just on the other side of this lie or that lie, that we'll finally be happy when this happens or when that finally arrives." Derek kissed the top of Jimmy's head. "Only to come out the other side of hell, beat up and battered like some old car, and find that heaven isn't a place at all. It's the ability to finally recognize the importance of perfect moments like this one."

"You should have been a writer," Jimmy said, looking up with a smile.

DEREK PRESSED his growing erection against the heat of Jimmy's entrance, amazed he was ready again so soon. He didn't do anything about it, preferring instead to just lie on top of his warm, sexy body.

Jimmy squirmed beneath him, trying to find a more comfortable position, and Derek took the opportunity to sneak one hand under the back of Jimmy's neck as he continued to study his handsome face and toned chest.

"I don't want you to go," Derek said, his voice a mere suggestion of a whisper.

"You know where to find me, where to send the letters, what number to call."

"Why couldn't I have met you instead of Beth?"

"Given what you've told me about your life at that time, you probably would have labeled me as a *fag* and ignored me."

"True," Derek sighed and brought their lips together. "Or maybe, just maybe, you would have been the one to make me see it was okay to be who I really was. I could have had you all this time."

"But you have me now," Jimmy said and snapped his hips upward, causing Derek's rock-hard cock to press against Jimmy's hole. "And it's only quarter to ten. So, given the shape of your incredible body, you could probably have me a couple more times before I have to go."

"Fuck me," Derek growled and raised himself so that he was on his knees looking down at Jimmy. He reached for another condom and the lube. "Get on your hands and knees, darlin'."

Jimmy did as he was told, and Derek lowered himself right away to rim that tight hole. He worked at it until Jimmy was moaning his name, over and over, pushing his ass into Derek's eager tongue. When Derek thought he would burst from the anticipation of taking him again, he put the condom on and lubed himself and Jimmy.

"Ah, yes," Jimmy sighed as Derek slowly pushed in, then grabbed Jimmy's hips as he pulled out. He snapped his hips and felt his entire length squeezed. Letting his eyes close and his head fall back, he was lost in the sensation of being surrounded by the heat of that hole.

"Yeah," Derek hummed over and over as he thrust in and out. He reached under, put his hand on Jimmy's chest, pulled him up, and leaned back so Jimmy was sitting on his cock. "Put some lube on that gorgeous cock of yours, Jimmy." Derek let go briefly so Jimmy could do as he was told. Derek took hold of the slippery shaft and began to pump slowly, up and down. With his free hand, he turned Jimmy's head and kissed him. Then Derek was back to moaning as Jimmy's contractions brought him to the edge.

"Faster," Jimmy demanded as he started moving his ass up and down on Derek's cock. "Make me come, baby."

"Yes, sir." Derek grunted and began pumping his hand faster and faster, making sure to squeeze the head of Jimmy's cock on each upstroke.

"Fuck," Jimmy yelled. "Yeah. Right there. Right there."

Derek tried to hit that same spot over and over and felt Jimmy's ass grip his prick tighter and tighter. "Come with me, baby," Derek said as he took his hand, wrapped it around Jimmy's neck, and began thrusting his tongue in and out of his ear, stopping only to whisper, "Come with me, Jimmy."

After another couple of thrusts, Derek felt the vice-like grip on his cock and knew that Jimmy wouldn't need much more before he started to spill his seed all over himself and Derek's hand. He let go of Jimmy's neck and cupped his balls instead, massaging them as his head fell forward to rest against Jimmy's sweat-slicked back.

"Fuck, yeah," Derek muttered as he felt the familiar sensation in his balls. "Come for me," he sighed as he rode out his own release. Moments later Jimmy muttered his own litany of profanity before relaxing back onto Derek's body. Derek leaned back on his heels, gripped Jimmy's torso in both arms, and turned his head so he could lick and kiss the shell of his ear.

Derek very slowly pulled out of Jimmy and reached for a tissue to dispose of the condom. He guided them both to the mattress and snuggled in behind Jimmy as their breathing returned to normal. "What time do you need to leave?"

"I should probably be on the road by one or two. I'll have to pick up Bozo and Miss Alicia."

"Will you call to let me know you arrived safely?"

"Of course."

"Make sure you're naked when you do."

Chapter 13

JIMMY WAS tired. He arrived back in town, picked up his babies, and headed home. He called Derek and had to leave a message since Derek didn't pick up. He unpacked, sorted his laundry, took Bozo out for a walk, and then played with Bozo and Miss Alicia for a half hour.

Finally Derek called just as Jimmy was settling himself in bed. They talked long into the morning hours. Jimmy felt sleep-deprived the next morning. But he still rose at the same time, still took Bozo out for his usual walk, and still made it to the bar to see if Ken had had any problems.

He found a handwritten note. All had gone well, nothing to report. He was relieved. He prepared the bar for the few regular customers who would be heading in, he assured himself that all the glasses were clean and that there were no pressing concerns to address, and then headed upstairs for a nap. No sooner was he on the bed than he felt the slight shift that came from eight additional legs traveling across the mattress.

He snuggled them close. The attention from the animals gave him some time to think about what had just happened to him. He was a reliable judge of character, so there was no regret about having given himself to Derek, or even about promising to be there for Derek in the months and years to come. It hadn't taken Jimmy long to realize that all of Derek's bravado of pickup lines and innuendo had been hiding something. Jimmy had spent so many years around sad and dejected people in his bar, not to mention all the people he'd come to know at the hospital with Bozo and Miss Alicia, that he recognized the smell of regret and resignation. But unlike some of those people, Derek had hope. After all, any man who found enough energy to keep coming back after multiple rejections was either hopeful or a deluded masochist.

Jimmy thought of Billy and his man coming to hear the band. Billy was like Derek—he still had hope. Sure, he talked like a drunken stalker and didn't seem to want to take "no" for an answer, but that just convinced Jimmy he was correct in his assessment—Billy was lonely and didn't know how to right the wrongs in his life. Like so many others, he sought comfort at the bottom of a bottle. He may or may not have helped Billy, but Jimmy lived under no delusions. Sometimes people took his advice, moved on, and made a difference. Other times people were just too comfortable accepting defeat.

"That's not me," Jimmy said to his babies. "And thank God, that's not Derek, either." He closed his eyes and let Miss Alicia's purring lull him to sleep.

"HEY, BOSS!"

Jimmy turned to see Ken walk into the bar, pulling off his sunglasses and smiling like the proverbial cat who ate the canary. "Hey, Ken, how you doing?"

"Great," Ken said. "Thanks again for the promotion."

"Not a problem," Jimmy said, wiping down the counter behind the bar for the fifth time. "Mindy didn't mind?"

"No. Not at all. In fact she told me to give you this." Ken came behind the bar and offered him a small blue tin. He didn't wait for Jimmy to open it, just started working on making room for the contents of the boxes he and Jimmy would be unloading in another hour or so. "Hope you like oatmeal raisin cookies."

Jimmy took the lid off the tin and peeled back a corner of the wax paper that covered the cookies. "I love them. Remind me to call her so I can thank her."

"Will do. Least I could do."

"Nonsense. I was happy to do it for you, Ken. You've more than earned it. In fact if you want to take some more time off, you just let me know, and I'll figure something out."

"Okay, thanks. But if you don't mind, I'll save another free weekend for about six months from now."

Jimmy put the lid back on the tin and turned to look at Ken, who was wearing the goofiest and proudest grin Jimmy had ever seen. "Seriously? You're pregnant?" Jimmy dropped the wet cloth and walked over to shake Ken's hand.

Ken shook Jimmy's hand and then hugged him. "I guess condoms don't always work. This isn't something we were planning, and it freaked me out at first, but—"

"You'll be fine," Jimmy said, unable to stop smiling. "You think you work hard now, just wait until the baby arrives."

"I know," Ken said, his smile fading a bit. "Was hoping I'd be in a better place by now, but…." Ken shrugged his shoulders.

Jimmy returned to the other end of the bar. "So, I guess that means Mindy will have to stop working within the next couple of months?"

"Don't know if we can afford it," Ken sighed, shaking his head. "I mean, of course she'll have to take maternity leave from school, but she's already planning on teaching during the first semester so we can save as much money as possible."

"Isn't that dangerous?"

"She's already spoken to her doctor, and she said it would be okay as long as there are no complications like higher blood pressure and working long hours."

"Well, then this is perfect timing," Jimmy said, throwing the cloth in the sink and leaning against the counter. "I've been thinking about taking some time off. You know, not being here as much, maybe doing some traveling around on the weekends."

"Good for you, Boss."

"So, looks like making you my new manager was a stroke of genius."

"All your ideas are genius, Boss."

Jimmy looked at Ken's smirk and laughed at the change in Ken. When Jimmy had decided to take a chance on him, Ken had been so nervous for the first month that he practically jumped every time he heard his own name. Not even a year later, Ken was one of the best workers the bar had ever seen. And he was more than patient with all of the men hitting on him every night. In fact Ken was a hell of a lot more patient with it than Jimmy.

DEREK GOT to his motel room, threw the suitcase on the first bed, and put his keyboard case on the second. He reached into his pocket, pulled out his cell phone, and paged through the dozens of pictures he'd made Julie, Suzie, Phil, and Nick take of him and Jimmy. He opened his backpack and reached for his blue stationery. He felt like sending Jimmy another letter. He checked his watch and was disappointed that it was only ten minutes later than the last time he'd checked. So, he kicked off his shoes, pushed his suitcase aside, and wondered what Jimmy was doing at that very moment.

His cell phone rang, but he didn't answer it right away. Instead he took a moment to listen to the song that Derek had come to think of as "their" song—"All That Heaven Will Allow," by the Mavericks. He sang along with it and wondered if it could be that easy—he would think of the man who'd completely captivated his every thought, the phone would ring, and Jimmy would be waiting patiently on the other end.

"Hello?"

"What the fuck, Derek?"

"Braden?"

"Oh, at least you recognize your son's voice. That's encouraging."

Derek closed his eyes and wondered if this little bit of contact with his eldest child was sparked by Beth or by the self-important brat himself. "What can I do for you, Braden?"

"Why the fuck did you tell Mom I told you the check was for the university?"

"Because you did."

"Fuck that. I did not."

"Okay, Mr. Nineteen-year-old Adult. You swear at me one more time, and I'm hanging up. Understand?"

"I *never* told you that the check was for tuition."

"I'm not arguing with you about this. You know you did, and so do I, and unless you want me to start recording our conversations, you have two options. Grow up and act like the adult the law says you are, *or* continue to act like a rude, entitled five-year-old and reap what you sow."

"What the fuck does that mean?"

"Good-bye, Braden."

"Wait!" Derek heard the sigh on the other end of the phone. "Okay, fine. I'm sorry. Happy?"

"I am," Derek answered. "But I'll be even happier when you admit you lied to your mother. You know as well as I do I would never send you a check for almost ten grand just so you could go and spend it on whatever you spent it on." Derek waited for a moment to let that sink in. "Firstly because I don't have that kind of money to waste. And secondly because you and I both know that I'm the only adult in your life who managed to save any money so you and your sister could go to college."

"What? So, Mom's done nothing for us?"

"Did I say that? Shall I repeat myself?" Derek sighed. "Listen, Braden, you want to keep up this act that I'm the worst father in the world, you go right ahead. But you are an adult now, perfectly capable of making your own way in the world. Last I heard you didn't get that part-time job that was part of the deal, you lied to your mother about the school not getting the check, and most importantly, you knew what you were doing was wrong, but you chose to do it anyway."

"So, what the hell do I do for tuition?"

"I don't know, Son. Perhaps you could sell whatever you bought with the ten grand I already sent you. I've kept my end of the divorce agreement and done without a lot so you and your sister could have advantages a lot of other teenagers will never have." Derek closed his eyes and counted to ten. "And by the way, you want to call me 'Derek,' as if we're somehow equals, start acting like it, and I'll allow it. 'Dad' is not good enough for you because you're pissed off at me and at life, fine. Then you can call me 'Mr. Roberts.'"

"Whatever."

Derek heard the click and waited for the dial tone. He flipped his phone shut and wondered how long it would be before it rang again. He didn't have to wait long. He smiled when he heard the ringtone, knowing it wasn't Jimmy but wishing it were. He thought of opening his phone to see the picture in which Jimmy was looking up at him, a huge smile on both of their faces. After the fourth ring, he opened his phone.

"Hello, Beth."

"That money's going to have to come from somewhere, Derek."

"I agree."

"Good. So you'll send another check."

"No, I will not." Derek smiled, thinking that the only thing that could make this day any more perfect would be if he were to hang up the phone and find a naked and writhing Jimmy waiting for him on the bed. "Our irresponsible and deceitful son could—"

"Deceitful? You want to talk about deceitful?"

"Go out and get a job. Or you could dip into that savings account you tried to hide from my attorney when you demanded half my salary during the divorce. Regardless of the option you and Braden choose, please understand that I'm done with these conversations. I've met *all* of my obligations as per the divorce, and I will continue to until both our children have graduated from university or college or whatever they choose. If you call me again about this, I will be more than happy to have my lawyer contact yours."

"Perhaps that is the only option," Beth said, her voice like needles in his ears.

"I agree—again." Derek took a deep breath. "But I would strongly recommend that you read the divorce agreement very carefully. I have met every one of my obligations, and you have met one or two. I don't think it would take a judge too long to figure out where Braden and Kelley's rude and hostile attitude about me comes from."

"Maybe they've just recognized you for what you really are?"

"And how would that be possible, Beth? They started refusing to visit with me within the first year of the divorce. Interesting that the reasons a nine-year-old and a seven-year-old gave were the same you gave when you filed to have sole custody. At least *I* find that interesting. So did the judge, if I recall."

"I'm serious about contacting the lawyers, Derek."

"So am I. In fact I'll contact mine tomorrow. You do the same. I'm done apologizing for ruining your life, Beth. It's been ten years. Time to move on. Good-bye."

Derek closed his phone, and the crisp blue stationery caught his eye. He smiled as he thought about how surprised Jimmy had been to receive the first letter. Derek had grown up long ago, in the days before the Internet and instant communication. He still thought letters were romantic.

He picked up the stationery and headed to the small table in the corner.

Chapter 14

"YOU OKAY, BOSS?"

Jimmy looked at Ken, whose expression was a mix of amusement and concern. "Yeah. Just a letter from a friend." Jimmy looked at the blue envelope. The postmark reminded him it had been almost a week since he'd held Derek in his arms.

"A friend, huh?" Ken went back to cleaning the glasses for the evening rush. "Last time I read something that made me turn ten shades of red, *and* that put a grin like that on my face, it was from Mindy. I asked her to marry me the next day."

"How's she doing, by the way?" Jimmy put the letter on the counter between himself and Ken.

"She's doing great. Well, other than the morning sickness."

"Baby's healthy, though?"

"Yeah, he's fine," Ken said and stopped cleaning, his eyes wide. "Shit," he said, finally. "Wasn't supposed to tell anyone."

"A son? You're having a boy?" Jimmy put a hand out and rested it on Ken's forearm.

"Didn't really care whether it was a boy or a girl, but...." Ken looked down as he picked up the next glass to clean. "I'm gonna have a son, Jimmy." Ken's voice was a whisper.

Jimmy couldn't be certain, but he thought he could see a tear or two forming in Ken's dark eyes. "Come here," Jimmy said, wrapping his arms around the tall, tattooed former biker. "You'll be a great father, Ken."

"Hope so," Ken said as he leaned into the hug. "Hope I don't mess that up too."

"Ken," Jimmy said, pulling away. "You've got a woman who loves you and a good job now. You've paid for your mistakes, paid your debt. All you need to do from here on out is to make sure your son knows how much you love him."

"Thanks, Boss."

Jimmy smiled. "And if there's anything I can do for you and Mindy, you just let me know. Okay?"

"Sure thing." Ken's mood seemed to lighten a little, and he cleared his throat. "Know it's none of my business, Boss, but I couldn't help but see the return address. Wasn't that singer's last name 'Roberts'?"

"I think so, yeah," Jimmy said, trying to slough off the topic. He lazily rifled through the rest of the mail.

"Mindy was pretty sure he was sweet on you."

"Really? Why would she think that?"

"Just a feeling she had. She was convinced that whenever he was singing, he was looking straight at you," Ken said, his grin seeming to indicate that Jimmy's evasiveness was only proving Mindy's theory. "He's a fine-looking man, Boss."

"What would you know? You're straight and married." Jimmy held up the periwinkle blue envelope and then slapped it back on the pile of mail. "Besides, this is probably a bill."

"Doesn't mean I can't recognize a good-looking man. And that envelope's a real pretty blue color. Can't remember the last bill I got in a pretty blue envelope, but I guess it happens, huh?"

Jimmy collected all the mail. "I'll be back in a couple of minutes."

"Okay, Boss. Take your time. You know, just in case you want to read that *bill* a couple of times."

Jimmy's smile grew more and more broad as he ascended the stairs to his apartment. He sat down on the sofa, and Miss Alicia made her way to him almost immediately. Bozo was still snoring at the other end, his head half buried under his favorite cushion. He studied the letter. First he looked at the handwriting—the bold, confident strokes, the rounded cursive writing. It brought back memories from his childhood. Letters from friends who had moved away and from his grandparents before they died.

He carefully pulled at the tongue. He wanted to save the envelope as well as the letter, so he stuck his little finger underneath the flap and separated the two pieces little by little. Jimmy felt as if it were Christmas morning.

He held the blue stationery stock up to his nose. Perhaps it was just his imagination, but he could swear he smelled Derek's cologne. It was intoxicating.

> *Hey darlin',*
>
> *I know you'll probably think I've lost my marbles, what with the Internet and cell phones and all the other ways to communicate with you. But I did warn you that I like to write letters. I can't stop thinking about you. Or our weekend together.*
>
> *It hasn't even been a full twenty-four hours since we parted, but I miss you already. I think you're the first man I've met in a long time who wanted to know the real me, not the Dizzy who sings just to get laid. I was surprised that you accepted my invitation to lunch. I thought I'd blown any chance of getting to know you better. And I'm still not sure what it was that made me recognize that the loss would have been all mine, but I'm glad you saw through the cheap lines and bravado. I'm glad about a lot of things since I met you.*
>
> *On the drive up here, I found myself thinking about all the things I'd wanted to do—to have—in my life. It's funny, isn't it, how focused we can become on one goal and not see so many of the others that we might have had slipping right by, until they're almost out of sight. At the risk of making you jumpier than a cat in a room full of rocking chairs, you're now one of those goals for me. I used to dream about being a good father, a good husband. I tried my best, but failed miserably. But I won't fail you. Seeing that smile on your face, hearing you call my name when we make love, these are the things that will fill the long nights without you.*

Give my love to Bozo and Miss Alicia.
Sleep well, darlin'.
D

DEREK ACCEPTED a Bud from a short, stout woman who reminded him that he had another set in thirty minutes. He raised the bottle in acknowledgment and downed half of his beer before heading back to Phil, who'd suddenly taken up smoking again. They were standing outside the bar when Derek felt his phone vibrate. He took it out of his pocket to see he'd missed a call from Jimmy. He smiled and put the phone back.

"Not gonna get that?"

"Later," Derek said, taking another mouthful of his Bud.

"You're done with your little twinks now?"

"You could say that."

"Well, well," Phil said, dropping his cigarette and crushing it with the toe of his boot. "Who would have ever thought that Dizzy would wise up?"

Derek just smirked and finished his beer.

"You're not getting any younger, or any prettier. Best put a ring on that finger as soon as you can."

"Nah, too soon."

"You're not fooling me, Diz. I've known you for many, many years, and I've never seen you like this," Phil said and opened the door to head back inside. "I'm happy for you, Diz."

"Thanks, Phil." He watched Phil retreat inside, took out his phone, and hit speed dial for Jimmy.

"Hello?"

"How's my darlin' tonight?"

"Sitting here reading a letter from an admirer."

"Well, shit. You mean I got competition?"

"No, I'm only one man's darlin'."

Derek could almost hear the smile on Jimmy's handsome face, and it made his heart skip a beat. "Music to my ears."

"How's your gig?"

"Going great," Derek said as he leaned against the building. "Going really well, but not too many beautiful blonds with piercing blue eyes and legs up to there for me to serenade."

"Thank you for the letter. It was very sweet. And I feel the same way, Derek."

"My pleasure." Derek cleared his throat. "Will you be available later?"

"Of course."

"Okay. I'll call you when I get back to the motel, say around midnight?"

"I'll be waiting."

"Talk to you soon, baby." Derek waited until Jimmy disconnected first, and then pocketed his phone. He thought he might have to write another letter that night.

JUST AFTER midnight, Derek sat on the bed, pulled out his phone, and dialed, a smile already on his face.

"Hey, darlin'."

"That's my line," Derek said, laughing. "How's the bar? You almost cleaned up?"

"Actually, yes. Ever since I made Ken the manager, he's been running this place like a German railway."

"How's he doing with being pregnant?"

"He'll be just fine. I think the part that's freaking him out the most is that Mindy's not freaking out."

Derek heard Jimmy laugh and closed his eyes, letting the sound wash over him like an unexpected rain shower. "It's an adjustment, that's for sure. So what're you gonna do with all this spare time now that Ken is taking over?"

"I was thinking of taking up letter writing, coincidentally enough. But since you move around all the time, I thought I'd use e-mail."

"I'm relieved that I'm not freaking you out with these letters." Derek put his head back and tried to picture Jimmy sitting on the sofa with his pets near.

"I love getting your letters. I used to watch old movies, and there would always be that one person who would save all the letters and wrap them with a ribbon or keep them in an old shoebox or something. I always wondered what it would be like to have that many."

"Did I just hear a challenge?"

"You can take that any way you'd like," Jimmy said.

"I miss you."

"I miss you too," Jimmy said. Derek could hear Miss Alicia purr in the background.

"How are the kids?"

"They're fine," Jimmy answered, but Derek could hear that something wasn't quite right.

"What's wrong?"

"Nothing," Jimmy said quickly. "Nothing with the kids. Mrs. Abramovich passed away on Thursday. Thursday morning."

"I'm sorry."

"I know you'll think I'm crazy, but I think Miss Alicia was disappointed not to be able to visit with her on Friday. I mean, she spent time with the other patients who wanted her to sit with them, but she kept going over to the same empty bed, over and over, and meowing. She never meows that much."

"I'm sorry, Jimmy. How is Miss Alicia doing now?"

"Oh, she's fine. She even got a card from Mrs. Abramovich's family. Sheila gave it to me when I was there on Friday. Her family wanted me to know how much comfort Miss Alicia brought their mother in those final days."

"That was nice of them," Derek said, wishing he could be there to offer more than words.

"It was very sweet of them. Miss Alicia got a special treat that evening—"

"And so did Bozo, I'm willing to wager."

"Of course," Jimmy laughed while Derek absorbed the sound, like a sponge. "And speaking of you thinking I'm crazy. I have something I need to say to you, and like your letter, you may not understand, but I really need to say this."

Derek was instantly alert. "What is it?"

"I know I have no right to say this, or ask anything of you that has to do with your previous life, but…. It upset me to hear you refer to yourself as a failure, and—"

"I don't think there's any denying—"

"Derek, you made a mistake, if you can even call it a mistake. You thought that Beth and the kids were what you wanted. You were wrong in the end, but I don't think that makes you a failure. You're a good, decent, hard-working man, Derek."

"Okay." He relented and let himself fall back on the bed. "I won't do that anymore."

"Good," Jimmy said, his voice soothing and filled with compassion. "And I need to say one other thing. Nothing you could say, over the phone, to my face, or in a letter will ever make me jumpy, Derek. I told you during our picnic that I knew there was something about you. And I also told you that I'll be here for you until you find whatever it is you're looking for."

"You're amazing. Simply amazing." Derek sat up and pulled his shirttails out of his jeans. He was still shaking his head, wondering what he'd ever done to deserve someone like Jimmy, when he heard the beep signaling another call. He rolled his eyes when he saw it was Braden and went back to listening to the sweetest voice he'd ever heard.

Chapter 15

"ANOTHER LETTER from your *friend*, Boss?"

"What?" Jimmy looked through the mail for the now-familiar blue envelope. There had been many of them in the last month; Jimmy had not seen Derek in exactly thirty days. "No, no letter today." Jimmy had figured Derek would write once or twice and then grow tired of it, preferring the convenience of a phone call or the relative ease of e-mail. But he was now averaging at least one letter a week, sometimes two.

"I'm sorry, Boss," Ken said, patting Jimmy's shoulder. "I'm sure it'll come tomorrow."

"No worries," Jimmy said, playfully poking Ken in the ribs. "He'll be here tomorrow night anyway, so...."

"I've already got earplugs," Ken said in a stage whisper, patting his shirt pocket.

"Very funny," Jimmy groaned. "I haven't seen him in almost a month. Those earplugs will *not* do you any good. If there aren't at least ten calls to 911 about the screaming, I've lost my touch."

"Or mind," Ken said. Then he dodged the flyers that Jimmy had just sorted from the mail and threw at him.

Jimmy's hip began to vibrate. He pulled out his cell phone. "Speak of the devil. Hi, Derek."

"Hiya, darlin'. Did you get my letter?"

"No, I just sorted the mail and didn't see it. Your darlin' is pissed off." Jimmy ignored the brief snort of laughter from his manager and started to head outside.

"Shucks, baby. It was my best one yet."

"I'll read it when it gets here. No worries."

"Or you could read it now."

Jimmy wondered what the hell Derek was doing. "It hasn't arrived. How am I supposed to read it right now?"

"Why don't you look again?"

Jimmy turned at the squeak of the front door. Bright sunshine obscured his view, but it didn't take Jimmy long to recognize those long legs and that sexy strut. With the phone still pressed to his ear, Jimmy ran over and threw himself at Derek, buried his face against his warm neck, and inhaled Derek's scent.

"I don't get a kiss?"

Jimmy pushed himself away only long enough to shove his phone in his pocket before taking Derek's handsome face in his hands and pressing their lips together. Their tongues met with a hunger that took Jimmy by surprise. Of course he'd missed Derek—missed holding him, kissing him, smelling him. He missed the feel of Derek's hands on his body and the sounds of sex with him. Each sound had a way of making Jimmy more and more determined to ensure they continued.

Jimmy pulled away when he needed air but left his hands on Derek's square jaw. "I'm sorry for that."

"For what, darlin'? Every man should get a welcome like that when he comes back."

Jimmy threw his arms around Derek's neck and laughed. "God, I missed you so much."

"I'd be lying if I said I hadn't thought about you once or twice." Derek kissed Jimmy's temple.

"Oh my God," Jimmy exclaimed. "That reminds me. You weren't supposed to be here until tomorrow."

"Nothing serious. Change of plans, that's all. I'm all yours for a whole week." Derek winked, and Jimmy thought he might tear the man's clothes off right there in front of Ken. *Oh, Jesus, Ken!* Jimmy led Derek to the bar.

"Derek Roberts, this is Ken. He manages the bar for me."

Derek put out his hand as Ken threw the towel over his shoulder. "Pleased to meet you, Ken."

"Pleasure's all mine, Derek. Boss, I can finish getting everything set up, so if you and Derek want to, uh, visit." Ken patted his shirt pocket again. Jimmy blushed.

"Where's Bozo?" Derek was looking around the room.

"Upstairs. Napping."

"Much obliged, Ken," Derek said, offering his hand one more time. "We'll try not to disturb you, but this one's a screamer, so…."

Ken laughed out loud and quickly regained control when Jimmy glared at him. At a loss for words and still blushing, Jimmy led Derek away from the counter. "Wait, where are your bags?"

"Seriously?" Derek put his hand in Jimmy's back pocket. "You want to do that now?"

Ken offered another snort, then coughed to cover it up and turned his attention to wiping the counter top. He was still smiling when Jimmy relented and led Derek up to the apartment.

"OH," DEREK said, patting Jimmy's ass as they headed up the stairs. "Here's that letter. Found it in your mailbox."

"Did not," Jimmy said as he took the blue envelope from Derek's hand.

"How do you know?"

"Because on the days when there's no blue envelope, I check a hundred times each day, just to make sure." Jimmy stopped in front of the apartment door, and Derek took his hand and spun him around. Derek's eyes were smoky with desire. He slid his free hand under the waistband of Jimmy's jeans.

"I wish I'd known, so I could write you every single day." Derek leaned down and pressed his lips gently against Jimmy's, bringing one hand to rest at the back of the shorter man's head. He pulled away when he needed oxygen. "Have I thanked you for the incredible week, yet?"

Jimmy sighed and stole another kiss before opening the door to the apartment. Derek went in ahead. Jimmy followed and closed the door then opened the letter. There was only one line:

There is nowhere else I want to be right now.

He looked up at Derek's sweet, nervous smile. "Derek," he whispered as he wrapped his arms around the taller man and accepted a tender kiss. "Wait here."

Jimmy disappeared into the bedroom, and Derek took the opportunity to greet Bozo, who was excited to see him. The Yorkie licked Derek and jump all over him, until he finally picked up the adorable mutt and carried him to the sofa. He wasn't sure what Jimmy was doing, but he told Bozo to stay put, and he did. Miss Alicia moved gracefully to sit on his lap, kneading his legs before she finally settled on a good spot.

"Sorry," Jimmy said when he reappeared. "I thought I had until tomorrow to make sure everything was clean and fresh in there."

"Jimmy, you know I wouldn't have noticed any of that. Not with you in there."

Jimmy picked up Bozo so he could sit down next to Derek, and the two of them pressed as close as they could. Jimmy kissed him, soft and slow at first, then pulled away. "I love my surprise, baby."

"Why I did it," Derek said, scooping up Miss Alicia and setting her beside his leg. He pushed up from the sofa and held out a hand for Jimmy. "Now I'm going to have a shower, and then I'm gonna get familiar with that body all over again."

"I've got a better idea," Jimmy said. He got up, deposited Bozo beside Miss Alicia, led Derek to the bedroom, and closed the door.

"But I smell like I've been in the car all day," Derek protested when Jimmy started removing his shirt.

"I don't care," Jimmy said, kissing and licking as he undid the shirt buttons and pushed the shirt off Derek's strong shoulders. "Nothing wrong with how you smell." Jimmy let the shirt fall to the floor, took off his shoes and socks, and then kneeled down. He looked up into Derek's eyes while his hands reached to undo the belt and then the jeans. "You smell like a man, a sexy, irresistible man."

"Missed you, darlin'. Missed this." Derek tenderly placed his hands on either side of Jimmy's head as he watched him pull down his jeans and then reach for the hem of his boxers. "Missed that sweet mouth."

Derek watched his erection spring loose and saw it engulfed almost immediately in that warm mouth. He closed his eyes as Jimmy cupped his balls with one hand and kneaded his left buttock with the other. He heard the moans he'd fantasized about, over and over, during those lonely nights in the hotel rooms. His breath was becoming ragged. If he didn't do something, this would all end far too soon.

He reached down and pulled Jimmy up so that the two of them were standing face-to-face. "Sorry, Jimmy. Been thinking about doing this for almost a month now." Derek quickly stepped out of his boxers and jeans and then moved Jimmy beside the bed. "Been thinking about your warm skin, the way you whisper my name when I do this." He pulled off Jimmy's T-shirt and tossed it on the pile already formed by his own clothes. He leaned down and kissed each nipple in turn, then brought his mouth up and pressed their lips together. He felt himself leaking precome and broke the kiss. "And this," Derek said as he undid Jimmy's jeans and slid both the denim and the briefs over his slim hips and strong thighs. Jimmy freed himself from his remaining clothing while Derek kissed him softly and intently.

When they were both completely naked and their erections were straining against each other, Derek reached down and took hold of Jimmy's ass and lifted him off the floor. "Wrap your legs around me. Hold on." After a few moments, he kneeled on the bed and lowered them both to the mattress.

"Derek, please." Jimmy was panting. He squeezed Derek's ass with his hands. "Waited long enough."

"Anything you want, darlin'." Derek pushed up onto his knees and stared down at Jimmy's flushed and willing body while he tried to reach the nightstand drawer for the condom and lube. He finally tore his eyes away long enough to find them and then returned his attention to Jimmy. "What do you want, baby?"

Jimmy raised himself up on one elbow and held out his hand, palm up. "I want you." Derek put some of the lube in Jimmy's palm and watched him wrap that hand around his cock. "I want to feel this beautiful cock fucking me, hitting my prostate over and over until I can't take it anymore and come all over myself." Jimmy lay back on the bed and spread his legs, then reached down to run his palm across his own hole. "I want you to get me ready. Stick your fingers inside me. Stretch me good before you do whatever you want with me."

Derek slicked his hand and bent over, doing as he was told. "You want me to start slow, pushing in and out?" Jimmy nodded. "Then you want me to go faster and faster until all I can think of is coming inside your tight ass?"

"I want you to do whatever you want, baby. It's your hole."

Derek closed his eyes and felt an intense wave of lust overtake him. He concentrated on pushing two fingers in and out, tickling Jimmy's prostate over and over, delighting in the sounds and the dirty talk. "You ready for me, darlin'?" Derek lined up and pushed in.

He watched Jimmy's eyes roll back and hugged his calves to his chest. Within minutes, Jimmy was a writhing mass of incoherent sounds, his muscles flexing and releasing as Derek's thrusts became more insistent. Derek took the opportunity to nibble and lick Jimmy's muscled calves and run his hands up and down the length of his legs. Jimmy cried out and took himself in hand.

"Fuck, yeah, baby," Derek said as he placed Jimmy's ankles on his shoulders and leaned forward. He thrust faster as he leaned over Jimmy's sweating body. "Come for me. Come just for me."

"Derek! Derek!" Jimmy was crying out his name as he shot his seed on his own chest.

It was a sight that brought Derek to his own climax. He grunted as Jimmy's ass clamped tight around his cock. He pushed into the heat of Jimmy's hole one last time and then squeezed his ass while Jimmy wiped sweat off his forehead and his chest. "Oh, fuck, fuck, fuck," Derek said as he collapsed onto Jimmy's body, sated and exhausted.

Derek shivered as Jimmy caressed and stroked his sensitive skin. "I've got you, baby," Jimmy whispered in his ear. "I've got you." He felt Jimmy's legs wrap around his waist and Derek lifted his head to look at his lover. His blond hair was matted to his forehead, and his eyes looked tired but alive. He had the most serene smile on his face.

Derek had never experienced anything so powerful and tender, so animalistic and gentle all at the same time. He kissed Jimmy on the cheek and then on the lips, lingering there for a moment while their tongues moved against each other. Derek then did something that he'd never done with any of his bedmates before. He leaned in close, his mouth next to Jimmy's ear. "Can't wait 'til we get to do this every night."

Chapter 16

ONE ENTIRE week. Derek was awake, staring up at the ceiling, wondering if he'd ever been this happy, or this lucky. Jimmy's tousled hair was tickling his chin, his hand resting on Derek's hairy chest. *I'm falling in love.* Derek was certain. He'd felt something similar with Beth. But what he was feeling for Jimmy was even more powerful. It was a sense of anticipation for everything that would follow. He had an entire week with him, for now. But if Derek had anything to say about it, a lifetime would soon follow.

He felt Bozo shift beside him and then watched as the Yorkie yawned and went back to sleep. Derek smiled and shook his head. *Was I ever this happy? Did I ever really doubt that I would find this?* Miss Alicia strolled in, jumped on the bed, and settled herself on his stomach.

"Did you brush your teeth?" Derek whispered when she finally settled and stared up at him. She blinked slowly and lowered her head to her forepaws. "Today's your big day, huh? You and Bozo are going to the hospital, right?" Another slow blink. "Do you think your dad will let me come along?"

"You can do whatever you want for the next week," Jimmy said, rubbing his eyes. "Morning, baby."

"Morning to you too, darlin'." Derek leaned over for a kiss. "Miss Alicia and I were just chatting."

"I heard." Jimmy shifted his position so that Bozo wasn't squished between the two of them. He rested his head on Derek's shoulder. "You should be sleeping, though."

"Kinda hard to sleep when I'm smiling like an idiot."

Jimmy laughed and shook his head. Then he kissed Derek's cheek. "You're going to spoil me, you know."

"Okay, I'll stop." Derek tried to hide his grin. He saw the confused look on Jimmy's face. "Didn't expect that, did you?"

"I have to admit, I would miss all the sweet things you say to me."

"Okay, I won't stop, then."

"It's not even seven. Why don't you try to get some more sleep?"

"Wasted effort if I did," Derek said, pulling Jimmy close. "Why don't you get some more sleep and we'll take Bozo out for a walk when you wake up again? Then we can take a long, hot shower. I'll take you out for breakfast and then we can come back here for a nap."

"And by 'nap' you mean?"

"We come back here to the bedroom. I take off your clothes. You take off mine. We kiss and touch and kiss and make love and kiss and make love again. And then we sleep for a couple of hours."

"Hmm," Jimmy said after a moment. "I've been doing it wrong all these years."

"Good thing I'm here, then."

"Yes," Jimmy said, his fingers tracing lazy circles over Derek's chest. "A very good thing."

"WATCH THIS," Jimmy said to Derek as Bozo made his way to the flowerbeds in the abandoned junkyard. "It's so adorable."

"What? Bozo?"

"Yeah, this is, like, his favorite place to go to the bathroom." Derek came closer and put an arm around Jimmy's shoulders as they both watched Bozo squat and then look at them. "Oh, look away, quick." Jimmy turned and then felt Derek come up behind him.

"Doesn't like an audience?"

"No, I think it's a territorial thing. You know, like a privacy thing, I guess."

"Gotcha."

"Wait for a moment or two, and you'll hear the strangest sound you've ever heard. That will mean he's done."

"Okay."

After a moment or two of Derek kissing the back of his neck, Jimmy heard the telltale sound of Bozo covering up his deposit.

"Is he whimpering?"

Jimmy nodded and turned to look at his dog. "He'd spend all day here if he could. There's just something about this place."

"I could too," Derek said as he left Jimmy's side and headed toward the rows of abandoned and rusted automobiles. "Look at all these great cars."

"Uh-oh," Jimmy sighed. "If you love cars, I'm afraid I'll need to do some reading before I can contribute to that conversation."

Derek laughed, returned to his side, and kissed his temple. "No worries, darlin'. My father was the car nut. But I guess some of it rubbed off on me. I used to help him restore cars. Even thought about taking it up as a hobby myself, but... well, you know my story— saving every penny and traveling so much."

"I'm sorry, baby."

"Don't be. I may still do it one day." Derek kneeled down when Bozo came back. He picked up the pooch and accepted some kisses before putting him back on the ground and rubbing behind his ears. "My father left me two classic cars—a 1953 Buick Skylark and a 1960 Ford Mustang. They were two of my favorites that we did together."

"They must bring back wonderful memories every time you look at them, huh? What a special thing to have to remember your dad."

"Yeah, it was," Derek said and stood back up, wrapping an arm around Jimmy again. "Had to sell them so I could keep up with payments to Beth and the kids."

"Oh, Derek, no," Jimmy whispered.

"Now don't go feeling sorry for me, baby. I did what I had to do to meet my obligations."

Jimmy pressed himself against Derek and leaned up to kiss him. It was a soft, gentle kiss of commiseration. Jimmy knew what it felt like to lose something so precious, to be left with nothing but memories of what should have been. He pulled back and looked up at Derek. "You didn't deserve that."

"The kiss?" Derek said, winking.

Jimmy grinned. "Life can really suck sometimes, can't it?"

"Sure can," Derek agreed, pulling Jimmy into a tight hug. "But then it turns around and leads you to the love of your life."

Jimmy pulled back once the words sank in. He looked into Derek's eyes.

"I love you, Jimmy." Derek kissed his forehead. "I kept telling myself to wait until the perfect moment, but they're all perfect when I'm with you."

"I love you too, Derek. I finally realized it when you showed up yesterday. Anyone who knows me would think I've lost my mind. I mean we've only known each other for a month, and we've only been together for *maybe* a total of three days. But I knew because whenever I'm with you, it's like my mind finally settles down, and I can think clearly."

"I'm making you a promise right now, darlin'," Derek said, holding a hand under Jimmy's chin. "I'll spend the rest of my life making sure you know just how much I love you."

Jimmy turned his head and kissed his palm. "Am I the luckiest man or what?"

"Second luckiest."

"SHEILA, THIS is Derek. Derek? Sheila." Jimmy watched as the two of them shook hands in the hospital lobby. It wasn't exactly nerves that produced the hesitation in his voice. He'd called Sheila that afternoon while Derek slept and asked her if it would be okay for Derek to come by the hospital. She said it would be fine as long as the two of them stayed together. He was nervous for the two of them to meet because Sheila was full of questions—which he'd declined to answer on the phone—and would be demanding answers fairly soon.

Jimmy noticed that Derek was keeping his hands to himself. No little touches to the small of his back. No standing too close. He had not once called him darlin'—only Jimmy—and was not even speaking unless either Jimmy or Sheila asked him a question. And he was even carrying Bozo while Jimmy held Miss Alicia's carrier.

"I have some news you may not like," Sheila said as they rode up in the elevator.

Jimmy felt the prickly heat climb up his spine, wondering what she meant. Were his visits over because he'd found a boyfriend? And even so, how would the hospital administration have found out so quickly? Could Sheila have said something after Jimmy explained about wanting to go away for that weekend to visit Derek and see where their relationship would go? He dismissed the idea as quickly as it came to him. Sheila would never do anything like that. He looked up at Derek, and his nervousness must have been evident, because Sheila elaborated.

"Not about you two. It's about Josh's parents."

"What's wrong?"

"Seems they've got their minds set on finding out who gave them that... present in the envelope."

"You didn't tell them, did you?"

"Not yet." The elevator stopped, the door opened, and Derek took a few steps to the right while Sheila whispered with Jimmy. "They would really like to thank you, sweetie."

"I don't know. You know how emotional I can get with things like this. What if I start bawling like a baby and make them feel even worse?" Jimmy heard the words and blushed to the tips of his ears. "I'm sorry. I know they couldn't possibly feel any worse, but—"

"Well," Sheila said, finally taking Miss Alicia's carrier in her right hand and holding out an envelope with her left. "They gave me this to give to you. Please? Think about it. Maybe it will help them in some way." She caressed his cheek and took a step back. "I'll go and get Miss Alicia settled. There's a certain grumpy old man who's been missing his cat. I'm sure he'll want to meet Miss Alicia."

Jimmy nodded and took the small envelope. He walked back toward Derek, turning it over and over in his hand.

"Does this mean I've got competition?" Derek said with a smile, pointing to the letter.

"What? Oh, no. Don't be silly." Jimmy leaned briefly against Derek's shoulder and absentmindedly petted Bozo. "Come on. The kids are waiting."

"Okay," Derek said, without any further discussion.

Jimmy felt like an asshole for dismissing Derek like that, but he didn't know what to do about the situation.

The two of them stood by the door and watched as Bozo made his way from one bed to the next, overjoyed to be the center of attention. He was sniffing and cuddling and as patient as always with the little kids, even when they insisted on braiding his bangs or making little ponytails.

"I'm sorry," Jimmy said softly. "I didn't mean to dismiss you like that."

"That's okay, darlin'," Derek whispered. "You'll tell me when you're ready. Although, I don't much like seeing you bothered like this."

"I'll tell you on the way home. I promise."

"Good enough for me." Derek pushed his shoulder against Jimmy's, trying to get him to smile. "You know, if I wasn't already in love with you, this—what you're doing right here—would have sealed the deal for me."

Jimmy said nothing, only looked up and offered a sincere, appreciative smile.

"Kinda unfair, you know?"

"What's that?"

"Can't help but think that I've got two perfectly healthy children who've never had so much as a cavity, and they're both the most selfish and—sorry," Derek said, lowering his voice even more. "And here are these little tykes fighting for their lives, and their faces just light right up at getting a chance to visit with Bozo."

"Life does like to play his little games, I guess," Jimmy said, shrugging his shoulders.

"Yeah, well, if I get my hands on him, I'll wring his neck—after bringing him in here and asking him to explain himself."

"There's no rhyme or reason, Derek. All we can do is whatever we can and hope they keep fighting."

"Wish I could bring those two spoiled little shits here. Probably wouldn't do any good."

"Whatever we can and hope, right?" Jimmy repeated. He led Derek to the geriatric ward to check on Miss Alicia.

"DID YOU want some more pie?"

"No, darlin', I'm stuffed." Derek was leaning back in his chair and rubbing his belly. "Can't believe the weekend's almost over."

"It's only Saturday," Jimmy said as he began to clear the dishes. "We've still got until Friday morning."

"I know, but I'm being greedy," Derek said, pushing himself up to help with the dishes. "And speaking of being greedy—how about I finish cleaning and you go and run us a nice hot bath. I have a sudden hankerin' to be naked with you."

"Sudden?" Jimmy laughed and pushed his hip against Derek's. "I think this is the first time we've been clothed in this apartment since you arrived."

"Yeah, but your body wasn't meant to be covered up, so lose the clothes, and I'll meet you in the tub." Derek patted Jimmy's ass and kissed his temple. "I even got some of them condoms we can use under water."

"Okay, boss, but you've seen the tub. You're going to be very uncomfortable in there if you're planning what I think you're planning."

"Challenge accepted."

"Okay, Gumby," Jimmy teased and began to walk toward the bathroom.

"I believe in this situation, I will be Pokey, if you know what I mean."

"Thanks for that. One of my favorite cartoons from childhood, and you managed to make it seem dirty."

"Would you prefer to be Nancy Drew and I'll be the creepy lighthouse keeper?" Derek laughed at the expression on Jimmy's face. "Or I could be—"

"Enough, I'm begging you."

"Not yet, but you will be."

Jimmy held up his hands in surrender and tried to block out the lascivious laughter from the kitchen as he walked to the bathroom.

"YOU DIDN'T fall asleep on me, did you?" Derek dunked the sponge under the warm bathwater again and squeezed it over Jimmy's chest, then watched as the rivulets of water made the spare blond hairs wave like flags in an afternoon breeze.

"No," Jimmy said. He stood, held out his hand to Derek, and helped him to stand as well. "But the water is getting cooler, so how would you like to join me in bed?"

"Hmm, I'll have to think about that."

Jimmy snorted as Derek took his hand and stood up. "Stay right like that," Jimmy ordered as he closed the sliding shower door, reached for the handheld showerhead, and turned the faucet. "Don't move."

Derek closed his eyes and enjoyed the hot water from the showerhead falling onto his head and making its way down his body. He could feel Jimmy's free hand glide over his skin. He turned around when Jimmy pushed against his shoulder, and then Jimmy ran his hand over his back and ass. He wasn't surprised to look down and see himself becoming hard again. It seemed to be a predictable condition whenever Jimmy touched him. "Houston, we have a problem." He turned back to face Jimmy and reached for the showerhead. He replaced it in the cradle and then began using both of his hands to smooth the hot water over Jimmy's skin. Jimmy was hard again within a few seconds. He kneeled and took Jimmy in his mouth while he gripped his own cock. But just as quickly, Jimmy was asking him to stop.

Derek stood up, and Jimmy pushed him into the corner of the shower. "I want to look at you when you come." He stared into

Jimmy's lust-filled eyes as he took hold of his erection and pulled slowly, thumbing his slit. Derek followed his lead and wrapped his hand around Jimmy's straining cock.

Derek moaned. Jimmy had one forearm braced against his chest and was looking intently into his eyes, as if Derek were a habitual criminal and Jimmy a cop trying to teach him a lesson. Derek didn't know what was going on. He had never felt this way.

"Look at me," Jimmy commanded before leaning forward and taking Derek's lower lip between his teeth. After a few moments, as Derek felt himself approaching the point of no return, Jimmy kissed him fiercely, much more forcefully than he had ever done before. Derek was breathing so heavily by then that it seemed his lungs would never feel full again.

He felt lost—but in a good way. Derek had always been the pursuer, the one in control of every situation. It wasn't a conscious decision on his part but rather just the way things usually turned out. He'd always figured it was because he was the older sexual partner, the one with more experience, perhaps. But this? This was igniting feelings in him he'd always thought would not be for him. Jimmy was taking charge, nipping at his chin, giving him orders. "Gonna come, Jimmy."

"Me too," Jimmy grunted. "Look at me."

Derek did so as the two of them rode out their releases, fingers squeezing and teasing until each man was spent and exhausted.

They embraced and kissed while the hot water ran down their bodies. Neither of them spoke for a long time.

"Time for bed, baby." Jimmy turned off the hot water. He stepped out of the shower first. When Derek followed, Jimmy started toweling Derek's thick salt-and-pepper hair and then worked his way down his tall, fit body.

"Yes, sir." As Jimmy reached his legs, Derek grabbed another towel and waited for Jimmy to stand up. "Allow me."

"I could sleep for a week," Jimmy said through a yawn as Derek focused on drying his lover's body.

"I'm that exciting, am I?"

"That's not the way I meant it."

"I know, darlin'." Derek stood up and stole a quick kiss from Jimmy's full lips. He threw the towel over the sliding doors and then took Jimmy in his arms. "Have I thanked you yet for the best day of my entire life?"

"I think I'm the one who should be thanking you."

Derek leaned forward and kissed him softly. He put an arm across Jimmy's shoulders, led him to the bed, and called to Bozo and Miss Alicia.

Chapter 17

"HOW MUCH you think they want for this place?"

Jimmy turned his attention away from Bozo's daily deposit in the abandoned flower garden and looked at Derek, who was surveying the entire lot with his hands on his hips. "Seriously?"

"Yeah," Derek said, raising one hand to shield his eyes from the morning sun. "I was thinking it might be a good place to call home someday."

"A junkyard?" Jimmy asked, laughing.

"Why not?" Derek walked over and let a hand rest at the nape of his lover's neck. "I mean, it's not much now, but I've been getting some ideas."

"Such as?" Jimmy wrapped an arm around his trim waist.

"I was thinking that the house is pretty much good to go. Maybe a few minor repairs here and there, but it's got really good bones. And then over here," Derek said, leading them to the space between the house and the heaps of metal. "Build a really nice huge garden with a special little section just for Bozo. And over there, on the other side of the house, a beautiful deck with a couple of water features and a fire pit for lazy, romantic nights. Just the two of us, hidden from the road, making love under the stars before we relax in our own hot tub, then head inside to sleep in our bed—a cool breeze blowing in through all the open patio doors."

Jimmy didn't know what to say. He hadn't thought beyond their next visit. "Wow," he whispered.

"Sorry, darlin'," Derek said as he kissed Jimmy's forehead. "I don't mean to freak you out, but I like to think about these kinds of things. Makes me happy."

"I'm not freaked out." Jimmy squeezed Derek's waist a little tighter. "I'm ashamed to admit that I've been preoccupied with when we'll see each other again, and here you're way beyond that."

"I love you. You love me. We know we'll see each other—maybe not as often as we'd like. So, I'm thinking of the day when I'll get to wake up to you every morning." Derek kissed his nose. "That's all."

"I do love you, Derek," Jimmy said, leaning up for a kiss. Then he took his time surveying their surroundings. "It does sound like heaven."

"It is right down the street from the Afterlife, you know."

Jimmy smiled and wrapped his arms around his man just as Bozo trotted over, looking to get in on the action. Jimmy let go of Derek and got down on his haunches to pick up his dog. "I bet you'd like that, wouldn't you, Bozo? You'd finally have your very own yard to poop in."

"Yup," Derek sighed. "Doesn't get much more romantic than that."

JIMMY WAS sitting on the sofa with Derek's head in his lap. They'd started watching the movie, but Derek had fallen asleep less than halfway through. Jimmy had turned the volume down and spent the past hour caressing Derek's hair and letting his mind wander. He thought about the plans Derek had so casually mentioned that morning. Buying the property and building a life together—just the two of them, with their own home in their own little corner of the world—frightened Jimmy a little bit.

He'd been cocooned in his little apartment for the past twenty years. It was his sanctuary, his respite from a world that had, most days, seemed to take more from him than it gave. But that had all changed when Derek walked into the bar. Derek hadn't asked him for anything. He just wanted to be with him, to spoil him, to make love to him, to hold him. Jimmy had never dared hope for anything beyond living his tranquil and solitary life, volunteering at the hospital, and surrounding himself with a few good friends. But sleeping on his lap was a man who was promising Jimmy a different life—a new life, with a new ending. And Jimmy had no intention of wasting any time at all in accepting.

Derek stirred and slowly opened his eyes. "Movie over?"

Jimmy nodded and bent over for a kiss. "I didn't want to wake you."

"Sorry, darlin'. Didn't know I was that tired." Derek sat up and rubbed at the stubble on his cheeks. "What time is it?"

"Almost dinnertime."

"Okay," Derek said, pushing himself off the sofa. "How about I shave and then take you out for a nice dinner?"

"Or," Jimmy said, drawing out the word as if it had five syllables. "I could take you out for a nice dinner. I mean, if you're serious about buying the junkyard, you'll need to start saving your pennies."

"That's true," Derek sighed, pulling Jimmy close. "What are you in the mood for?"

"You mean food?"

"Careful, darlin'," Derek warned. "I'm never too tired for you."

Jimmy laughed. "Don't I know it. Well, let's see. It's Wednesday night, and you're an omnivore, so we could go to Chester's. There's a surf and turf that Ken always raves about."

"Sounds good to me." Derek started walking toward the bathroom but stopped and turned. "Do you need to be in the bar tonight?"

"Nah," Jimmy said. "Ken can handle it for an hour or two. Besides we were both there Monday and Tuesday, and I think it kinda drove my new manager a little crazy having so many people trying to help out."

"That's probably just you. Ken and I had a nice chat last night."

"Oh?"

"Yeah," Derek said, leaning against the wall by the bathroom. "It kinda felt like he was asking me my intentions toward you."

"What?" Jimmy furrowed his brow. He quickly removed his T-shirt.

"That's what it felt like." Derek crossed his arms over his chest. "Of course, considering what you did for him, I guess it's right he'd feel kinda protective."

"He told you?"

Derek nodded. "Told him not to worry, that I'd take care of you. Make you happy."

"I can't believe he told you about his past."

"We all got one, darlin'. Some of us just had a few more bumps and detours than others."

"You're a very wise man, Derek Roberts." Jimmy unbuttoned his jeans and disappeared into the bedroom. "Now, get washed up, because I'm starving."

"HOW'S MINDY?" Jimmy was standing behind the bar, hands on hips, looking at the crowd.

"She's fine," Ken said as he finished mixing a gin and tonic and placed it on the bar in front of a very attractive blonde woman. She handed over a few bills and winked at Ken when she told him to keep the change.

"If you turn this into a straight bar, I'm gonna be pissed."

"Wait for it," Ken said, and Jimmy followed his gaze.

The woman returned to a table near the stage, placed the drink in front of another equally attractive woman, and then gave her the most passionate kiss Jimmy had seen since... well, since Derek had thanked him for dinner. "Sorry," Jimmy said, stifling a laugh.

"It's their ten-year anniversary tonight. They're from out of town, on their way to visit the brunette's parents. Father's not doing very well."

Jimmy threw up his hands in defeat. "How the hell do you do that?"

"It's a genetic thing. Navajo's are natural charmers." Ken winked and leaned a hip against the bar. "I think Derek must be part Navajo."

"Part?"

"Well," Ken grunted and shrugged a shoulder. "He's not as charming as I am."

"Jesus Christ," Jimmy moaned as he saw Ken's smile. "I don't know if I can handle two of you."

"I like him, Boss." Ken held out his arms. "I'm real happy for you, Jimmy. He's a really great guy, and he's head over heels for you."

Jimmy obliged his manager with a quick hug and then patted him on the shoulder. "Thank you, Ken. I appreciate that." He started to head back upstairs to Derek but turned at the last moment and walked back to Ken. "You know I didn't mention anything about your past to him, right? You know I would never do that."

"I know," Ken said, raising his arms to redo his ponytail. "I just wanted him to know everything about me, so he wouldn't worry about you when he's away from home."

Jimmy suddenly felt overwhelmed. He had two completely different men in his life, and each of them wanted to protect him. He headed back upstairs and found Derek asleep on the sofa with Bozo on his lap and Miss Alicia on his chest.

I'm home. Jimmy suddenly realized he'd never thought of this space as anything other than an apartment.

JIMMY WAS awake and staring at the ceiling. Derek's head rested comfortably on his bare chest. He looked at the clock. In another four hours, Derek would have to leave for his next gig. He closed his eyes and tried to think of the past week with this incredibly sweet man. It wasn't working. All Jimmy could see were the upcoming days he would spend sleeping alone and eating alone. He didn't want to go back to that. He wanted Derek all to himself, each and every day. But he knew he had no right to ask Derek to tour less, to sacrifice a dream he was finally able to live, just because his boyfriend was lonely. He would have to resign himself to accepting whatever time they would have together.

Derek snuffled and lifted his head. "Come here," he said, as if he knew what Jimmy was thinking. He shifted onto his back and pulled Jimmy with him, guiding his worried head to rest on his strong shoulder.

"Go back to sleep, baby. You've got a long drive ahead of you."

"I'll be fine," Derek whispered before reaching for Jimmy's hand and placing it on his chest. "I'm gonna miss this," Derek said as Jimmy's fingers began to tease their way through his thick chest hair.

"Maybe I can come out to be with you again?"

"I'd love that, darlin', but it's too far. I don't want to be worrying about you driving for ten hours just to see me."

"But—"

"If something happened to you, I'd never forgive myself." Derek kissed the top of his head. "And what would happen to Bozo and Miss Alicia and the bar and all those wonderful kids who depend on you?"

Jimmy knew Derek was right, but the next few gigs would mean they wouldn't see each other for a couple of weeks. He opened his mouth to mention that but closed it again. Then he closed his eyes and tried not to cry.

"I'M SORRY," Jimmy whimpered, wiping at his eyes. They stood, each in sweatpants and a T-shirt, by the junkyard house. The bright sunshine was just another cruel contradiction for Jimmy. If it had been a cloudy, cold day, he wouldn't feel so betrayed.

"You gotta quit apologizing, darlin'." Derek was holding him, stroking his back. "You got nothing to be sorry for. I'll miss you too. More than anything." Derek placed his hands on Jimmy's shoulders and looked into his eyes. "We'll be together again, real soon. I promise."

"I know," Jimmy said, trying to get a grip on himself. "I guess I'm just a lonely old queer, huh?"

Derek wrapped his arms around him again and sighed. "What you are, Jimmy, is mine. All mine."

Bozo came trotting over, as usual, and Jimmy bent down to pick him up. He held him in his arms while the Yorkie licked his face.

"I stand corrected," Derek said. "You're ours."

"I'm not trying to spoil this for you."

"Nonsense," Derek said, putting an arm over his shoulders and guiding them back to the street. "Can't remember if I've ever had someone cry because I was leaving before. Had plenty people cry when they saw me coming, but—"

Jimmy laughed and swatted at Derek's chest. "I told you not to talk like that anymore."

"I was just trying to make you laugh."

"I know. And I'm sorry you had to."

"Come on. I wanna make love to you one last time before I have to be on the road."

They returned to the apartment, and Jimmy prepared breakfast, although he wasn't hungry enough to eat anything. He picked at the food on his plate, trying to cheer himself up so Derek wouldn't worry about him.

"I've got something for you," Derek said after he finished his bacon and eggs. He stood up, walked to one of the little tables beside the sofa, opened the bottom drawer, and pulled out a familiar blue envelope. He returned to the table and handed it to Jimmy.

Jimmy opened the envelope, careful not to rip it.

>*My darlin' Jimmy,*
>
>*When I was just a boy, I remember asking my father about marriage and what it was that made a mom and a dad want to spend their lives together. He did his best to explain about love and the feeling of butterflies whenever he thought of mom and spending the rest of his life with her, but I guess I was still too young. I would lie in bed and cry some nights when I realized that I wouldn't always be in the same comfortable bed, wouldn't always go to sleep surrounded by the same wallpaper full of cars and motorcycles, wouldn't always wake up to my mom's smile and her telling me that she and daddy loved me.*
>
>*I was too young to understand that my dad was telling me that one day I would meet someone whose happiness meant more to me than my own, someone whose very existence meant that mine had meaning. I looked for them for a long time, and even thought I'd found them once, but I was always disappointed. I always wanted to go back to that comfortable bed and see that old wallpaper and my mom's smile.*
>
>*But then I found you. And I realized it wasn't the bed, or the wallpaper, or mom's smile that I wanted. It was that feeling—the one my father had described—that feeling of butterflies and wanting to spend the rest of my life with someone. I'd never known that feeling, until you.*
>
>*I love you, Jimmy. I love your quiet, reserved nature, and your strong, determined mind. Despite your*

past, you reach out and help people—Ken, Mindy, Sheila, Bozo, Miss Alicia, and those brave, sick children. I love how you look so peaceful when you're sleeping. I love how you touch me, kiss me, hold me. I love how you sigh just before you put your head on my chest and fall asleep.

I finally understand what my father was talking about. I finally understand that there will never be anyone for me but you. I understand that everything in my life has brought me to this place, this moment. To you.

Nothing will ever change how I feel about you, Jimmy. I have what I've always wanted.

Derek

Jimmy read the letter twice, wiped the tears off his cheeks, and looked up to find Derek crouching beside his chair. Derek stood up and took Jimmy with him. He held him tightly as Jimmy caressed his cheek.

Neither of them spoke for a few minutes. Jimmy was trying to regain some composure when Derek finally whispered in his ear, "I'll always come back to you, darlin'."

"You'd better," Jimmy said through his sniffles.

Chapter 18

"OKAY, YOU'VE got the list with all the numbers?" Jimmy asked, setting down his suitcase and backpack.

"Yes, Boss. Everything will be fine." Ken smiled at Jimmy, probably trying to show his boss that there was no reason to worry.

But Jimmy was worried, more worried than he was the last time he left the bar to go and see Derek. He would be gone for an entire week, traveling with Derek to two different gigs. He'd been foolish enough to mention the idea to Ken, never realizing that he would be totally fine with it. "I'm telling you, Boss. If a man of mine did that for me while I was missing him like Derek misses you, there'd be no doubt in my mind I belonged to him." Jimmy laughed and promised Ken he would never tell Mindy about Ken's "man."

But as the time drew closer, Jimmy realized he didn't need to control everything at the bar. Ken had proven himself over and over again. And as for Bozo and Miss Alicia, Sheila had immediately volunteered to keep them for a week. In the end Jimmy found himself with no excuses and an overwhelming desire to be beside Derek.

"Boss? It'll be fine. Go be with your man."

Jimmy smiled, suddenly nervous about leaving his fur-babies. He'd dropped them off at Sheila's earlier in the day. It wasn't that he didn't trust her, because he did. Jimmy imagined Bozo and Miss Alicia calling for him, looking for him, their eyes sad and resigned when he didn't come. He was torturing himself with these thoughts even though he knew he was being ridiculous, but it was only the second time they'd been parted since he rescued them.

"Come on," Ken said as he scooped up Jimmy's bags. "You're gonna miss your flight."

"If you need anything, just call me, okay? Doesn't matter what time it is." Jimmy was making his way to the car, still wondering what he was going to do during the two-hour flight.

"I'll be fine, Jimmy. I know what I'm doing." Ken put the backpack on the front seat and then stowed the suitcase in the back. "I had a good teacher."

"And you have Jill's number in case you need to be with Mindy?"

"Boss," Ken said, gripping Jimmy by the shoulders. "You're gonna make yourself so sick with worry that you won't be able to enjoy being with him." Ken released his grip and smiled at Jimmy. "Just picture the look on his face when you show up."

Jimmy nodded one final time and got behind the wheel. Ken didn't move. Jimmy rolled down the window. "Thank you, Ken. I apologize for making you think I don't trust you."

Ken waved a hand dismissively and folded his arms over his chest. Jimmy pulled the car into reverse and backed up before heading to the highway. With one final wave, he was off for a week-long vacation, something he hadn't had since purchasing the bar twenty years before. And Jimmy was most surprised that it was because of a man—a man Jimmy loved with all his heart.

DEREK STOOD at the back of the bar with the other members of his band, waiting to be introduced. The sound check had not gone well and had eaten away all of his time—time that he had wanted to use to call Jimmy. They had never been apart for such a long time, and Derek was finding it a special kind of torture.

They had settled into a romantic routine of phone calls. Derek was still trying to express what he was feeling in letters. He wanted to make sure Jimmy understood how much he cared for him. But nothing would ever replace being able to touch and kiss and hold the man who'd given Derek so much while asking for so little himself. Jimmy would be arriving the next day at noon, and then they'd have a week together. Jimmy would be on the road with the band.

But Derek wasn't sure it was all worth it. He'd become more and more preoccupied with the thought of that little house—and restoring cars and making love under the stars.

Phil put a hand on his shoulder and pushed. They were on.

Thoughts of Jimmy, although never far away no matter what Derek was doing, sat alongside his routine of singing and banter. All he had to do was imagine that Jimmy was out there, looking at him with those playful blue eyes that promised nights full of passion and devotion.

The band had really started to gel. They'd been touring and playing for almost a year, and their hard work was paying off. Each set was tight and clean, each song hitting the mark as the crowds cheered and danced. Derek often thought the credit belonged to Jimmy, that his little darlin' had brought some peace and resolution to his scattered and confused emotions. They had featured his ex-wife and his children for too long. But not anymore. Derek finally knew what it meant to be in love, knew what it meant to love someone else. He'd even written that letter explaining it all to Jimmy.

During their first break, Derek was with Phil behind the bar. Phil was still smoking, although he promised to stop again since his crystal-clear tenor was showing signs of distress. Derek was out for the fresh air. He preferred it to being inside with Clark, who was as unpredictable as ever.

"Things okay with Jimmy?" Phil had always been supportive of his relationship with Jimmy. "Only stupid people turn their backs on a chance at love," Phil had told him only the week before.

"Yeah, sure. Why?"

"You seem a little distracted," Phil said, stubbing out his cigarette before he'd finished half of it.

"Not really. Just thinking on some stuff."

"Like what?"

"I love him, Phil." Derek shook his head and smiled. Hearing himself admit it for the first time made it seem real and frightening. "There was always something there, right from the beginning, you know. And we both knew that it might fizzle out, but…." He shrugged. "But that man is who I think about every minute of every day."

"But that's a good thing, right?"

"Of course," Derek said quickly. "It's just… I don't know how much longer I wanna be without him. Christ, Phil, that's no way to treat a man as good and generous as Jimmy. He deserves better than what I've been giving him. I wanna marry him."

"So, what? You wanna leave the band?"

"No, of course not," Derek said just as quickly. "But if I do leave the band so I can be with him, what the hell am I gonna do with myself? Restore cars at our junkyard?" Derek noticed the confusion on Phil's face, so he explained about walking Bozo and the discovery of the abandoned lot, complete with what could be their own little hideaway.

"Have you talked to him about it yet?"

Derek shook his head, feeling like a coward. During their last visit, he'd started to ask Jimmy if he was happy, if he was content with being together once or twice a month. But the words died in his throat. He put on a brave face for Jimmy, promising to always return to him, but inside Derek felt like he was using him. Giving the man a quick fuck, whispering a few words in his ear, and then taking off again, to do what he wanted to do.

"Well, do that first, man. Maybe you're worried about all this for nothing."

Derek nodded and followed Phil inside to finish the gig.

JIMMY STOPPED at the hotel to drop off his luggage. The young man at the front desk had some trouble keeping the smile off his face when Jimmy announced who he was. "Yes, Mr. Campbell. Mr. Roberts let us know that you would be coming. No, Mr. Campbell. It's not a problem that you're early. I'm sure Mr. Roberts will be very pleased to see you."

The taxi dropped him off, and he headed into the packed club. Jimmy hadn't told Derek he had arranged to be on an earlier flight. He patted his back pocket to assure himself that he'd remembered his wallet so he could pay the cover charge.

The heavy aroma of sweat, smoke, and spilled beer hit his nostrils moments before he heard that familiar voice singing about all that heaven will allow. He paid the cover charge and walked to the bar, cursing himself for having missed most of the show. He had thought he'd be in time to hear Derek singing their song. And he'd even fantasized about Derek spotting him in the crowd—a big smile would transform his handsome face and he would tell everyone that he was singing this song to his little darlin'.

Jimmy waited for the song to end and asked the bartender for a Bud. If he managed to do this right, he would have a drink waiting for Derek by the time he realized that Jimmy was there to surprise him with his early arrival. He paid for the beer and leaned against the bar.

"Hey, sweet thing. You lookin' for some company?"

Jimmy turned around and saw a tall, thin unkempt man standing beside him. "Oh, no, thank you. I'm just waiting for someone."

"Well, no worries, darlin'. I'm here now. No need to wait."

Jimmy tried to smile but realized from the look on the man's face that he probably hadn't succeeded. "I'm already someone's darlin', so please leave me alone."

"Ah, come on, baby. I can show you a good time."

Jimmy saw the hand move across his shoulders and then felt it on his ass. With one swift movement that came from years of working in his own bar and heading off potential disasters caused by men who wouldn't take "no" for an answer, Jimmy reached around and took hold of the man's thumb. He turned to face him and pressed his thumbnail into the drunk's cuticle. "I'm sure you're a lovely person, but I am not interested. Do you understand, or do I need to get that very tall, very muscular bouncer?"

The man tried not to look as if he was in pain but failed miserably. "Okay, sugar. You don't need to tell me twice."

"Thank you," Jimmy said as he watched the man mumble something under his breath and walk away. When he turned to face the stage, Jimmy saw Derek heading toward the back of the bar. He grabbed the Bud and headed in the same direction.

He caught Phil's eye and held a finger to his lips—a silent request for Phil to say nothing while Jimmy sneaked up from behind. "Hey, Diz," Jimmy said, trying to disguise his voice. "There's some good-looking blond darlin' out there who bought you a Bud."

Derek turned, wiping the perspiration off his forehead. His eyes grew wide and Jimmy laughed and held out the Bud. Phil, probably sensing what Derek would do, swooped in and took the beer seconds before Derek picked Jimmy up and kissed him senseless.

Chapter 19

DEREK WAS sitting on the edge of the bed, tired but utterly ecstatic that Jimmy was with him. When he saw him the night before, Derek thought he'd finally lost his mind. After picturing that face and that sexy body in the audience as he sang their song night after night, Derek figured he'd blown a fuse in his brain and had some sort of meltdown. But he hadn't.

He walked to the bathroom and glanced back at Jimmy, debating whether or not to let him sleep. He flushed the toilet, washed his hands and face, and was brushing his teeth when Jimmy walked slowly into the bathroom—naked. Derek finished brushing his teeth and moved aside to let Jimmy brush his, but he couldn't keep his hands off the warm skin of Jimmy's back.

"Have I thanked you yet for my surprise?"

Jimmy nodded and reached out to pet Derek's belly. When he was done washing up, Jimmy led Derek back to bed. "I think we might need some more sleep."

"No way, darlin'," Derek said as he held the sheets back and watched Jimmy crawl under them. "God, you're just the finest thing I've ever seen, Jimmy." Derek got into bed and wrapped Jimmy in his arms. "I got some things I want to say to you. I've been wanting to say them for a while now, but it just didn't feel right in a letter or over the phone."

Jimmy lifted his head and looked him square in the eyes. "Okay."

"You know I love you. You know I promised that I'd always come back to you."

Jimmy sat up and looked down into his face. "What is it, Derek? You're scaring me."

Derek coaxed Jimmy back into his arms. "Sorry, darlin'. I just don't want you to think this is your fault." Derek saw Jimmy's mouth open again, but he continued. "I'm leaving the band. I want us to buy that junkyard and fix up the house and make love under the stars and give Bozo his own little flowerbeds to fertilize."

Jimmy sat back up, again. "But you love performing."

"I know, but I've had ten years of that. I'm saving the rest of my time for you." Derek's left hand caressed his smooth back while his right moved the hair off Jimmy's forehead. "And I'm swearing to you right now that I'm yours if you want me. For as long as you want me. All yours. Only yours." Derek took Jimmy's hand and kissed the palm. "I've still got about four more months of contracts to fulfill, but after that it'll just be us—together. No more snatchin' a few days here and there."

Jimmy sat cross-legged on the bed, running his hand through his hair over and over again.

"Hey, darlin'," Derek said, sitting up and taking Jimmy's face in his hands. "Did I say something wrong?"

"No," Jimmy said. "No, Derek. What you said is perfect."

"Then what's wrong?"

"What if you resent me? I don't want to be the reason you quit the band."

"'S okay, darlin'," Derek said, his own eyes filling with unshed tears at the thought of what Jimmy must be feeling. "I'm not doing this because of you. I'm doing this because this—us—means more to me than spending all my time on the road with no home, no family, no you."

Jimmy studied his face and then kissed him softly, tenderly. "You promise you won't blame me?"

"I promise, Jimmy."

"I love you. I'll be with you no matter what you decide." His hands found Derek's, and with their fingers interlaced, Jimmy kissed him, gently at first. Derek lay back down and pulled Jimmy with him.

Jimmy straddled Derek's slim hips and brought their clasped hands over Derek's head. They kissed for several more minutes before Derek pushed against Jimmy's hands and guided him onto his back. He was still between Jimmy's thighs, and he pressed against his firm ass as he brought his knees up, preparing for another round of lovemaking. Derek's erection grew more and more when he let Jimmy's words wash over him.

"WOULD YOU stop?" Jimmy swatted playfully at his chest and Derek grabbed his hand. "As long as I'm with you, that's all that matters to me."

"I can call him and cancel," Derek said, squeezing Jimmy's hand and letting it go.

"Don't you dare. You said you guys have never played this city before, so maybe he doesn't know anyone either." Jimmy picked up an earthenware jar in the shape of a Yorkie. "If you cancel I'll be very upset with you." He turned the jar over in his hand. "I guess this is a treat jar for dogs, huh?"

"Bozo would love that. I'm gonna buy it for you."

Derek reached for the treat jar but Jimmy pulled it away. "Bozo drinks out of the toilet. Do you really think he'll appreciate that his treats now come out of this?" Jimmy put the jar back on the shelf, and Derek laughed.

"How are the babies?" Derek moved closer, slipping his hand into Jimmy's back pocket.

"They're wonderful, as always." Jimmy turned to face Derek, a shy smile on his face. "They're as helpful and charming as ever. Bozo's become quite attached to a four-year-old girl. She's been diagnosed with cancer."

Derek sucked in a lungful of air through his clenched teeth. "Poor baby," he said, pulling his hand out of the pocket to settle it on Jimmy's hip. "And my son thinks it's a life-ending crisis that he has to have a part-time job to pay for his deception."

"They'll come around, Derek. You just need to give them some more time to realize that the world doesn't revolve around them."

"I'm not worried so much about Kelley. But Braden?" Derek sighed and picked up a tug-of-war rope. "Last I recall Bozo's was falling apart. You haven't gotten him a new one, have you?"

"No," Jimmy said. "I thought you said Beth and Braden had been dealt with already, through the lawyers."

"Oh, they have, but I'm just hoping Braden'll learn the right lesson from this experience. There's always the possibility that this will make him even more deceitful and conniving to get what he wants."

"That's what I don't understand." Jimmy watched as Derek put the rope in the basket near his feet. "Even if only half of what you tell me is true, both of your children have had plenty of opportunities to spend time with you, but they've refused time and again."

"Never underestimate the determination of the embarrassed ex-wife of a once-closeted police officer." Derek studied a package of furry mice. "You know, I don't remember ever seeing Miss Alicia play with toys."

"Oh, she does," Jimmy said, turning and pointing to a brightly colored display of nylon cubes. "She's more into agility stuff than swatting things around. Remember. She's a therapy animal. She's not aggressive or mean to any living thing."

"Ever?" Derek wrapped his arm around Jimmy's shoulders, and Jimmy slipped a hand under his waistband. "Speaking of aggressive."

"Sorry." Jimmy picked up the basket of goodies and winked. "I'm finding it really hard to keep my hands off you. I keep thinking about what's underneath that T-shirt and those baggy jeans."

Derek reached into his back pocket and pulled out his cell phone. "I'm canceling, and we'll get room service."

Jimmy laughed and took the phone away, offering one kiss to appease the beast he'd unleashed. "I promise I'll be good," he said as he slid the phone back into Derek's pocket. "Although when I think about what that perfect ass of yours must look like when you're pumping inside me...." Jimmy turned and started toward the checkout, whistling to himself.

"This is not an attractive side to you, you know," Derek whispered as he came up and goosed his lover. "Saying things like that, knowing I'm not wearing any underwear. I'm gonna have to carry the bag in front of me all day."

"I'll make it up to you," Jimmy said, stepping in front of him and reaching around to pat Derek's hip. He wanted to turn around and see

Derek's flushed cheeks and wide-eyed stare but knew that if he did, they were never going to make it to lunch.

"You have no idea how much."

"NICE TO see you again," Phil said to Jimmy.

"And you," Jimmy said. He shook Phil's hand and then sat across from Derek. "I've heard some wonderful things about you."

"Likewise," Phil said and picked up his menu.

Derek moved his foot next to Jimmy's. He looked down at the menu when Jimmy smiled at him. "I think I'll have the burger and fries," Derek said after. "My stomach can be a bit sensitive before performances."

"Oh, Jesus, I'd forgotten about Barrowhill," Phil said, rolling his eyes. "Our first gig," Phil said, turning to Jimmy. "Everything is set. We'd been rehearsing for weeks. Ten minutes before we're to go on, but I can't find this one anywhere. I'm starting to sweat bullets, wondering what the hell we're gonna do without vocals and keyboards, only to find him hugging the toilet in the men's room."

Derek watched Jimmy bite down on his bottom lip, his expression a strange mix of sympathy and amusement. "Everything turned out fine." He turned to Phil and squeezed his elbow. "It's not like you've never caused some problems, buddy."

"Like what? I'm the consummate professional!"

Derek snorted and looked at Jimmy. "Ask him about Bellwyn."

Jimmy turned to look inquisitively at Phil, who was glaring at Derek. "I was drunk," Phil said, as if nothing more needed to be explained.

Derek took a deep breath and looked at Jimmy. "Mr. Suave, here, has his eyes—which until his surgery had required corrective lenses—on this 'smokin' hot man's man' all night while he's up on the stage. Mr. Over-forty, however, doesn't want any of the hot young things to know he's old enough to be their father, so he doesn't wear his glasses. As the night wears on, he's making eyes and flirting and drinking. So much drinking going on that he's unaware that the smokin' hot man is a powerlifting lesbian."

"Oh, my…." Jimmy's eyes were wide, but he did not laugh. "Did she have a sense of humor?"

"He wouldn't know. He was unconscious after the first punch."

"Why did she punch you?" Jimmy looked from Derek to Phil and back again, probably realizing that Phil was not about to provide the details.

"She's obviously offended, but Mr. University-graduate looks her straight in the eye and says, 'Nobody's perfect, honey. We'll figure it out by morning.'"

Derek leaned back in his chair and took in Jimmy's muted laughter. *Jesus, but this man is everything I've ever wanted.* Derek watched Phil fall under Jimmy's charms.

"I'm so sorry, Phil," Jimmy said, reaching a hand out to rest on the man's forearm. "But what did that even mean?"

"I wish I knew," Phil said, as a smile finally crossed his flushed face. "Best thing that happened to me, though. How I met the man I've been with ever since."

Jimmy looked over at Derek. "Skip was one of the orderlies who helped repair Phil that evening."

"Oh, that's so romantic," Jimmy said. "Obviously, Skip is a man of excellent taste."

"Thank you, Jimmy. Now, what do you see in this old, broken-down fag?" Phil asked, turning to push Derek back in his seat.

"Asks the man who can't tell men from women," Derek said, leaning forward again and resting his elbows on the table.

"That's a very long list," Jimmy said and looked at Derek with tenderness. "But at the top of that list would be his incredibly generous heart."

Derek moved his other leg against Jimmy's, trapping both of them between his own. *Love you,* Jimmy mouthed.

Derek smiled and responded in kind, wondering what else was on that list.

"YOU'VE DONE this for ten years?" Jimmy fastened his seatbelt and started the car.

"Yup."

"God," Jimmy muttered, shifting again. "I can't feel my ass anymore."

"I'll give you a massage when we get to the hotel." Derek reached over and let his hand rest on Jimmy's right leg. "And if you don't behave, I'll only use my hands."

They stopped at the gas station to fill up and to get some bottles of water and a package of Goobers for Derek. It was Jimmy's turn to drive, and after almost seven hours, they were still hours from their destination—a midsize town, the name of which Jimmy had already forgotten, that would see Derek and the band play three nights in a row. After that town there would be another two-day trip to the big city of Warkentin. It would be Jimmy's final stop before flying home alone.

"I meant to ask you before," Jimmy said as he headed back to the highway. "Does Skip come out on the road with Phil ever?"

"No. Well, maybe once or twice a year."

"How does that work, exactly? I mean, Phil obviously loves him a great deal. But don't they miss each other?"

"They're like us, I guess." Derek squeezed Jimmy's thigh. "Sneaking in whatever time they can, making it count."

"What will Phil do when you leave the band?"

"He's been talking for years about maybe starting his own band, one that doesn't tour, but just plays local gigs, so he can be with Skip more."

"So he's not upset about you maybe leaving?"

"Hasn't said anything if he is."

Derek sank down and closed his eyes. Jimmy wished he had some kind of reassurance that Derek was making the decision to leave the band for himself and not for any other reason. But it seemed that every time he brought up the topic, Derek told him not to worry about it and changed the subject.

Chapter 20

"Happy three month anniversary," Derek said, reaching into the drawer of the motel nightstand and taking out an intricately carved wooden box wrapped with a single blue bow. Jimmy had arranged to be at another gig, this time traveling only two hours to spend the weekend with Derek.

Jimmy looked up, took the box in his hands, and caressed the carvings. It was a beautiful scene of two people standing by a river, their arms around each other.

"Reminded me of our first picnic behind the bar, by the river."

"It's beautiful," Jimmy said, tearing his eyes away from the carving. "I don't have anything for you."

Derek laughed and wrapped his arms around his lover. "Now that's the most ridiculous thing I've ever heard." His kissed Jimmy's temple and whispered in his ear. "Every day I get to remind myself that you love me."

"I do," Jimmy sighed, turning his head to kiss him.

"It's taken me fifty-one years to find you, but it was worth the wait." Derek kissed his temple again and looked at the box. "Open it."

Jimmy thought the box was the present, but he pulled off the ribbon, opened it slowly, and peered inside. Nestled in a piece of purple crepe paper was a rectangular piece of pewter attached to a key ring. The rectangle was engraved with their initials at each cardinal point, like a compass.

"Turn it over."

Jimmy saw the engraving—*All That Heaven Will Allow*. He opened his mouth to say thank you, but the words caught in his throat.

"If you start crying, then you know I'll turn into a blubbering fool."

Jimmy laughed and wiped at his eyes. "It's absolutely perfect." Jimmy kissed him, hoping his lips could convey how happy Derek had made him. "Speaking of presents," Jimmy said as he gently put the key ring back in the box. "Will you be able to make it home for Thanksgiving? And Christmas?"

"The boys and I decided to take two weeks at Christmas, and we've booked a gig about an hour away from you for Thanksgiving."

Jimmy exhaled and threw his arms around Derek, kissing his way up his strong neck to his sensual, full lips. "I'll make it memorable. I promise."

"Darlin', you just need to show up for that to happen."

"And I'll be sure to test everything beforehand, make sure I can cook everything just right, so you'll have a traditional holiday feast. For Thanksgiving *and* Christmas."

Derek took the box out of Jimmy's hand and stood in front of him. He eased Jimmy back to lie on the bed. "I already give thanks every day for the present I got three months ago. But if you wanna do that for us, I'll be sure to thank you in your favorite way, each and every night."

Jimmy caressed Derek's solid biceps and triceps as Derek moved himself so he was lying on top. He stared into Derek's eyes, hypnotized by the sparkle and the mischief. "I need you, baby."

He wanted to memorize everything about this moment. Sex with Derek was always incredible, and now they were planning their future months in advance. Jimmy had no doubt in his mind that Derek was the love of his life, and even though he found that thought exhilarating— finding love at this time in his life—he also knew it would mean sacrifice. He would have to learn to live with Derek being gone for weeks at a time. And while that would be frustrating, Jimmy was not about to complain about one minor flaw in the otherwise perfect life ahead of them.

Derek raised himself on his knees and began to unbutton his shirt. Jimmy trailed his index finger over the ridges and indentations of his abdomen, then combed through his soft, luxurious chest hair. Derek gently pulled Jimmy to a sitting position and pulled off Jimmy's shirt.

"I wanna take my time," Derek said. "I won't see you again for another three weeks."

"I'll always wait for you," Jimmy said, rubbing his face against Derek's stubble.

Derek pressed their lips together, and Jimmy moaned and parted his lips willingly. "Is the stubble okay? Does it hurt?"

"No."

DEREK'S SKIN felt like it was on fire. He had offered his future to Jimmy, and Jimmy couldn't seem to get enough of him. Derek was going to make sure that this night would be unforgettable for both of them—not only because they wouldn't see or touch each other for almost a month, but also because Derek needed to show Jimmy just how much his life had changed since they met.

He kissed his way down Jimmy's chest and torso but looked up when he heard a gasp. "What's wrong?"

"Nothing," Jimmy muttered, his voice low and raspy. "Your beard."

"I knew I should have shaved," Derek said.

"No. Do it again." Jimmy put his hands on either side of Derek's head. "It's rough on my skin and then you kiss it. God, Derek, it feels so amazing."

Derek smiled and lowered his head. He caressed Jimmy's taut belly with his chin and then kissed it. "Like that?"

"Oh, fuck, Derek."

That was all the encouragement he needed. He pressed his hand against his lover's straining erection, and Jimmy bucked to increase the friction between his cock and his jeans. "How 'bout we get these off?" Derek didn't wait for an answer. He snapped them open and pulled, alternating between the rough caress of his stubble and the softness of his kisses at each newly revealed section of skin. "Almost there, darlin'."

Jimmy lay with his hands above his head, grasping the sheets. He called Derek's name over and over and writhed when Derek finally exposed his engorged cock. He gasped when Derek took it into his mouth, once again alternating between rough cheek and the softness of his tongue.

"Hang on, Jimmy. I wanna try something." Derek continued to lower the jeans, inch by inch, caressing with his cheek before kissing and licking. He would have to remember these sensations on the cold, lonely nights ahead when he would be alone.

He released Jimmy from the confines of the jeans. As soon as Jimmy's long legs were free, Derek put his hands on the back of his lover's knees and pushed them up. "Tell me what you want." He leaned in and first pressed his stubble-covered chin into Jimmy's perineum and then kissed the same area, licking and blowing to cool the skin. "What will make you come for me?"

"That," Jimmy grunted. "God, I can't think. More, please."

Derek smoothed his hands over the backs of Jimmy's quivering thighs, rubbed his cheek and chin along his inner thighs, and then returned to his perineum and scrotum—each time being careful to kiss and lick the same area in turn. Jimmy continued to moan with pleasure and begged for more. Derek finally reached Jimmy's entrance and first kissed and then gently rubbed his cheek and chin against the puckered flesh. Jimmy almost jackknifed on the bed and let out a litany of grunts and expletives. "'S okay, baby. I got you," Derek said, over and over as he pressed on the backs of Jimmy's thighs as if he were trying to keep him from getting away. "I'm gonna get you ready."

"God, fuck me, Derek."

"I will, darlin'. I don't think you want it too bad, though. I need you to tell me how bad you want it."

"I want you, baby. I need it, right now. Please, take it. It's your hole. All yours."

"All mine, huh?" Derek licked at the hole, spitting occasionally to watch the rosebud quiver as it opened and closed for him. He felt his own erection straining against his jeans and reached for the lube and a condom. "That makes me the luckiest man alive, then, 'cause that's the tightest, sexiest hole I've ever had. Just for me, huh?"

"Yes. Uh-huh. All yours."

Derek ripped open the condom package, made quick work of sliding it on as far as it would go, then popped the top on the lube and slicked himself and Jimmy. "Open up for me, darlin'," Derek whispered as he put in the first finger. "I'm gonna get you nice and slippery." He introduced a second finger and then leaned over Jimmy and braced himself with one arm while he brought their mouths together and pushed two fingers farther and farther inside. He worked them in and out until Jimmy was ready.

He settled the tip of his cock against Jimmy's hole and stared down at his flushed body and hungry eyes. He was spellbound at the sight of Jimmy pushing himself, little by little, onto his cock. "Slow down, baby," Derek said as he pushed himself in to the hilt. "There's no fire. We got all night. And if I get my way, we're gonna do this over and over—"

"Stop teasing, please. Fuck me. Fuck me," Jimmy began to yell. He reached forward, grabbed Derek's ass, and dug in his fingers to demonstrate the speed and rhythm he needed.

"I'm sorry, darlin'." Derek leaned forward and rubbed his rough cheek against Jimmy's, whispering in his ear as he began to increase the speed and intensity of his thrusts. "Hang on, baby. You got me so excited, I know I'm not gonna last." Derek pressed his lips to Jimmy's ear and kissed it over and over, occasionally licking and teasing. "Can you—"

"Oh, Jesus, Derek. Fucking Jesus Christ."

Derek felt the heat on his belly, felt the muscle contract and squeeze his cock until he could barely thrust anymore. "I love watching you when you let go like that, darlin'." He kissed Jimmy's ears, cheeks, neck, lips, eyes—anything he could reach. The grip on his cock loosened just enough for him to get friction against the sensitive head of his cock, and he thrust hard for one final time, squeezed his ass muscles, and buried his head against Jimmy's neck. "Shit, Jimmy," Derek said, squeezing his eyes shut and emptying himself into the condom. "Closest I've ever come to fucking my brains out."

He heard a chuckle, felt soft wisps of air against his shoulder, followed by soft kisses and the tender caress of Jimmy's hands over his sweaty back. "Thank God you've got a lot of them, then."

Derek smiled and raised his head. "That was...."

"Yeah," Jimmy sighed. "It was."

Derek pulled out, and Jimmy pushed him onto his back and shimmied down the bed until he was between his legs. He kissed his way to Derek's scrotum, licking and nipping gently.

"It's too soon, darlin'. I'm not twenty anymore."

"It's not about that," Jimmy said, finally taking Derek's softening cock in his mouth.

Derek put his hands behind his head and was mesmerized as Jimmy licked and cleaned him.

"You always spend so much time on me," Jimmy said between licking and pinching his foreskin. "And you never ask anything of me. But just then? I don't think I've ever wanted anyone as much as I wanted you."

"That's 'cause I wanna please you. I wanna make you happy."

"I know," Jimmy said as he crawled up Derek's body and came to rest on top of it. "And it's never taken for granted, believe me. But I think it's time I started learning what makes you lose control and beg for more."

"Ah, darlin', that's easy. If you're in the room, I lose control. And if you're naked, I'll beg as long as you want me to."

"That's not what I meant," Jimmy said, laughing and snuggling against his warm body.

"I know," Derek said. "Let me put it this way—making love to you, knowing that you love me? That makes me lose control. Knowing that we'll be here together, just like this, with you in my arms and your head on my pillow? I'll always beg for more of that."

Chapter 21

JIMMY PUT his wallet in his back pocket, grabbed the plastic bottle of Fresca, and thanked the young girl behind the counter. He was only fifteen minutes from home but figured he should fill up on gas so he wouldn't have to do it later. The Fresca was an impulse buy—a treat because he'd managed to leave Derek without too much fuss and upset.

He'd been able to hold back the tears until he was outside the city limits, but then it had finally hit him that he wouldn't be hearing that voice, feeling those hands, or waking up next to Derek for three weeks. He would have Thanksgiving dinner to keep himself busy—both the test run and the real thing—but that was little consolation for the first seven hours of the drive. Now that he was so much closer to home, he was starting to feel a little less alone.

He would be back with Bozo, Miss Alicia, Ken, and the regulars at the bar. And he had Derek's present. He took it out of his shirt pocket and held it again, as he'd done at least a hundred times in the previous seven hours. Before he started the car to leave the gas station, he turned it over and over in his hands. He'd long since memorized every detail of the hand-carved wooden box that sat on the passenger seat.

With a sigh, he put the key ring back in his pocket and started to think about what he would get Derek as a present. He'd need one for Thanksgiving—and not just because he figured Derek would probably have one ready and wrapped—but also for Christmas.

They had talked about Derek getting a dog, one that he could leave with Jimmy or take with him if he wanted. But choosing a pet was a very personal thing. Jimmy didn't want to take the joy of choosing away from Derek. Of course he could take Derek to a shelter to find a dog. Then the present wouldn't really be a surprise, but another animal would have a home by Thanksgiving and Christmas.

Jimmy sighed in frustration as his mind traveled down well-worn ruts in the road that he had carved during the long drive home. Eventually he turned off the highway and stopped at the bar to drop off his luggage before heading to Sheila's to pick up his fur-babies. He grabbed his luggage and the wooden box and headed into the bar.

"Hey, Boss!" Ken was standing behind the bar, cleaning and organizing.

"Hi, Ken. Any problems?"

"Not a one," Ken said, pride evident on his face.

"You get the deposits to the bank?"

"Check."

"I miss the deliveries?"

"Yup. I've already stowed everything in the back room, *and* I rotated the stock."

"Sorry," Jimmy said as he deposited the luggage by the bar and put the wooden box on the counter. "I didn't mean to grill you like that."

"Not a problem," Ken said, putting down the glass in his hand and throwing the towel over his shoulder. "Whatcha got there?"

Jimmy saw Ken studying the wooden box. "It's okay, you can pick it up if you'd like." Jimmy leaned against the bar and reached into his pocket to pull out the key ring. "They're both presents from Derek."

Ken took the key ring in his hands and turned it over and over, studying first the initials and then the inscription. He whistled. "So when you gonna put him out of his misery and marry him already?"

"We haven't even talked about that. Besides, he hasn't asked me."

"Why don't you ask him?"

"It's all still so up in the air. I mean, he still has another month of gigs. And even then I don't know if he'll actually be able to give it all up." Jimmy looked up to see the hesitant look on Ken's face. "Sorry, I'm tired."

"Not at all," Ken said, resuming his cleaning duties. "I know you're the owner, Jimmy, but that don't mean you can't think of me as a friend."

"Thanks, Ken," Jimmy said as he picked up the key ring and put it back in his pocket. "The same goes for you. And Mindy."

"Boss? You mind if I ask you a personal-type question?"

"Depends, I guess."

"I've never asked anyone in the bar about you. Not the other staff or the regulars like Billy. But I overhear some of the men wondering about why you've never had a steady man before Derek."

"It's complicated, Ken."

"Sure. I'm sorry. Didn't mean to pry."

"No, it's not that." Jimmy settled onto one of the bar stools and took a deep breath. "My father was... abusive to me. Mom had already died, and I guess, I don't know, Dad sorta... fell apart. He died when I was twenty, and you could have knocked me over with a feather when the lawyer told me that Dad had left me a lot of money. I mean, more than I ever thought we had. Anyway, long story short, I bought this bar with a man I was seeing at the time, but he turned out to be worthless, and he spent way too much money. I almost lost the bar. Right then I promised myself—no more men who couldn't support themselves. And between running the bar and a lack of such men, I kinda got used to being by myself."

"Wise decision," Ken said. "Boss? I'm happy for you. I know I shouldn't have, but I've told Mindy a few times that I'm worried about you. Your whole life seems to be the bar, and...." Ken held up a hand. "Sorry. For someone who didn't want to pry, I seem to be doing an awful lot of it, huh?"

"It's okay, Ken," Jimmy said, hopping off the stool. "And thank you. I'm very happy I met Derek too."

"Brains, responsible, hard worker, and he's real nice to look at too."

Jimmy laughed and headed for the door. "You know, Ken, that's the second time you've told me how handsome Derek is. You sure you're straight?"

Ken laughed, and Jimmy pushed his butt against the door to open it. He steered himself toward the car so that he could go and get Bozo and Miss Alicia.

"HEY, DARLIN'."

"Derek," Jimmy said softly when he heard his man's voice on the other end of the phone. "Are you done for the evening?"

"Yes sir," Derek said. "Just got back to the hotel room."

"You didn't go falling for any roadies now, did you?"

"No sir. I already have the perfect man who loves me."

"Yes, you do. In case I didn't thank you enough this weekend, thank you for the incredible weekend. And my presents."

"My pleasure, baby." Moments of that weekend had played nonstop in Derek's head all day—the way Jimmy had given himself over and over, the look on his face when he opened his presents, the kindness and attention he'd shown Phil during lunch, asking him questions about Skip and generally making him feel like part of their little family.

They shared a few moments of silence on the phone, and Derek was more than happy to sit and listen to Jimmy breathe.

"I was looking through some cookbooks this evening, thinking about Thanksgiving," Jimmy finally said. "Is there anything special you'd like for Thanksgiving dinner?"

"Well, let's see," Derek said. "When I was a kid, I always loved the stuffing my mom made. She always told me that her secret ingredient was bacon. And I loved cranberry sauce. And pumpkin pie, of course."

"I just realized, Derek. In all the times we've been together, I've never asked about your family. I mean, I remember what you wrote in that letter—about your dad telling you about love and what it meant—but I'm ashamed to admit I've never asked you more."

"It was a pretty normal childhood, I'm afraid. I was decent in school but by no means gifted. My dad was a plumber and Mom was a teacher. Kindergarten."

"Brothers or sisters?"

"No, just me."

"We're both only children? What a coincidence."

"There's a lot of us, I would imagine. I was never supposed to be born. Doctors told my mom that she would never be able to have children."

"You must have been quite a surprise for them."

"Oh, yeah," Derek said, laughing. "In more ways than one. They were proud of me and all, but I think Dad expected me to go into a trade. So when I became a cop, he was a little confused, considering all the trouble I got into when I was a teenager."

"You know, I can imagine that. I can just see you trying to use that charm of yours to get yourself out of whatever trouble you caused."

"You're not far off," Derek said. "I used to do some pretty stupid stuff to get attention from the girls."

"And that was when you developed that whole routine? The one you tried on me the first time we met?"

"More or less," Derek said, cringing at the memory of how Jimmy had seen right through him and put him in his place. "Glad you were able to see through that act, darlin'."

"Me too," Jimmy said with a sigh. "I was standing there, listening to these lines, one after the other, and I kept thinking, why is he going to all this trouble? He's handsome, obviously smart, got talent. Does this routine actually work?"

"Like I said, I'm glad you called me on it," Derek said and cleared his throat. "It was a pretty lonely way to go through life."

"I can imagine. I chose the other path. You know, never letting anyone in? And it was pretty lonely too."

"Well," Derek said, wishing he were sitting beside his man. "Luckily, that's all over, for both of us. *And,*" Derek said for emphasis. "It looks like I might be with you for a lot longer than we'd planned at Christmas."

"What? Why? Are you okay? Is something wrong with one of the other band members?"

"Hold on," Derek said, chuckling to himself. He imagined Jimmy jumping up off the sofa or the bed or wherever he was, caught between pacing and racing to his car. "It's Clark. He's been thinking of starting his own band. If he does, the rest of us will have to decide whether to end it all right then or find a drummer and fulfill our contracts."

"You scared me. I mean that's terrible news for the band, but if Clark thinks he'll be happier doing his own thing… and if it means I'll get to wake up with you for longer than just the holidays, I won't be complaining."

"I've never heard you complain about anything," Derek said, his voice full of admiration. "That's one of the things that made me fall head over heels for you."

"When will he let you know?"

"We don't have anything booked for after Christmas yet. Nothing in writing, anyway. So I told him he'll have to let us know by the end of November, so we can find a new drummer."

"Are we still on for Thanksgiving? I mean, is that why you let me know?"

"What? Of course. Nothing's gonna keep me from you or that dinner. I was just telling you so you would be prepared for having an extended house guest at Christmas, that's all."

"Okay, sorry. Didn't mean to overreact."

"Quite all right, darlin'." Derek cleared his throat again. He tried to make his voice as sexy as possible. "Now, how about you and me have one of our special chats?"

Jimmy laughed. "I'm heading to the bedroom right now."

"Good. 'Cause I spent all day replaying last night, and I want to tell you about some other things I plan on doing to you next time we're naked together." Derek was out of his clothes in seconds.

He plopped back on the bed, already hard, and pictured Jimmy's body, warm and willing, stretched in front of him. He took himself in hand and heard Jimmy's husky voice come across the other end of the line. "I'm ready, baby."

Chapter 22

DEREK STOOD beside his car, checking for the final time to see if he had everything. He went down the list that included his luggage and his keyboard as well as the flowers and present for Jimmy. He was excited and didn't want to forget anything. Jimmy was an hour away, and they would be spending five days together. Five incredible, uninterrupted days of eating the Thanksgiving meal Jimmy was preparing just for him, walks with Bozo along the river, and talking about whatever until late into the night. Most important, they could make love whenever they wanted—without the need for a phone.

Satisfied that he hadn't left anything behind, Derek checked his watch one last time. He would arrive just before noon, giving them plenty of time to walk Bozo and make love. Then Derek would head to the hospital with his new family for Jimmy's regular Friday visit. He hadn't been this excited when Beth had agreed to marry him. But that was probably because Derek hadn't felt the same kind of sexual connection he had with Jimmy.

He slid into the driver's seat, started the car, and rubbed his hands together at the chill in the air. The highways weren't icy, and the trip would be relatively uneventful except for the fog that had rolled in overnight. It was dissipating slowly, but Derek didn't want to be late. He didn't want to disappoint Jimmy. *Ah, who am I kidding? I'm the one who'll be disappointed if I don't see him soon.* He still couldn't quite believe all of this was actually happening. He'd been so caught up in his life of touring and fucking anything that looked his way that he hadn't realized, until he met Jimmy, that it wasn't too late to have what he'd always wanted. He had thought he would have it when he married

Beth, but that happiness had been short-lived. Beth saw getting married as a reason to stop working and stay home. Derek saw it as a reason to see himself as a straight man.

But when he proposed this time, Derek knew he'd be doing it for all the right reasons. He loved Jimmy, and Jimmy loved him. There was a possibility that Jimmy might reject the idea of marriage, but Derek was tenacious if nothing else. And if being on the road turned out to be one of the reasons for Jimmy's rejection, Derek would stay in one place and find a job that would keep him home. He could always play on weekends. There was nothing Derek wouldn't promise to make Jimmy his and his alone.

Derek had argued with himself ad nauseam, about whether three months and three weeks was too soon to consider marriage. But Derek was certain his feelings would only intensify with time. So they could wait until their feelings were even more intense, or Derek could ask him right away and surprise the hell out of him—and they could celebrate Christmas as a married couple.

Derek had told himself that he would never again even consider marriage. When his relationship with Beth ended, he realized that his next partnership would be with a man. But the memory of his marriage was enough to steer him into a life filled with casual, anonymous sex. He thought he would grow out of it, but he let himself get lost in the counterfeit feelings that each anonymous encounter offered. He was no longer the reliable, contributing member of society who had received countless commendations for his work as a police officer. He was not the member of a band who wrote some of their music. He wasn't even a person with hopes and dreams. He woke up to realize he'd become nothing more than a hung, fifty-one-year-old adolescent Casanova who was wanted for his impressive endowment and his ability to fuck on command. He'd fought his despair until he met Jimmy.

Derek pulled the car to the side of the highway and leaned over to root around in his knapsack, certain he'd packed a bottle of water. He heard the squeal of tires and looked up to see where the sound was coming from. He saw nothing in front of him and quickly twisted around to look behind—just in time to see the out-of-control eighteen-wheeler a few yards from hitting his car.

Derek closed his eyes and thought of Jimmy.

JIMMY CHECKED his watch and walked to the door of the bar one more time. He had to leave for the hospital soon, and Derek still wasn't there. He should have arrived hours ago. There'd been no phone call, no message on his phone, no e-mail, nothing. There were dozens of reasons racing through his mind, but Jimmy kept trying to latch on to the simplest and least painful reason for Derek being so late. He ran into car trouble, and his cell phone battery was dead. He would call as soon as he was able.

"Boss?" Ken was standing behind the bar. Jimmy thought he was trying not to look concerned for his boss's sake. "You've got a lot of people waiting on Bozo and Miss Alicia. Why don't you go, and I'll call you the minute I hear anything."

"It's just so unlike him," Jimmy said, reaching down for the carriers. "He was so looking forward to another visit at the hospital."

"The minute I hear anything at all," Ken repeated and smiled, nodding his head. "Scout's honor."

"Okay," Jimmy sighed and lugged his two therapy pets to the car.

The drive to the hospital was uneventful, as usual, and Jimmy made his way into the hospital and waited at the front desk until Sheila exited one of the elevators.

"Hi, sweeties," she said, coming up and giving Jimmy a hug. "There's a new patient in geriatrics. She's been here for a few days and been missing her cats at home something awful. When I told her about Miss Alicia, she lit up like a Christmas tree." Sheila took Bozo's carrier and escorted them to the elevators.

Jimmy raised the cat's carrier and cooed, "Hear that, Miss Alicia? There's someone new who you can purr for."

"And what about you? Did Derek make it in okay?" Sheila held the elevator open.

"No, he hasn't arrived yet," Jimmy said, dismissively. "It's probably nothing. Probably got caught in traffic." Jimmy had told Sheila about Derek several weeks before when he'd decided to surprise him with a visit. He had to ask Sheila to take care of his visit for that week, and felt it was only fair to tell her the real reason.

"Have you called him?"

"Yes, but it just keeps going to voice mail."

"And you left a message?"

"Three."

"Well, when I want to get Edward to return my calls, I usually have to make them unspeakably filthy," Sheila said with a saucy wink.

"So the trick is to get him all worked up so he'll call you back?"

"No, he hates those kinds of messages," Sheila quipped, her eyes filled with mischief. "Calls me back to remind me he hates them. Works every time."

"You're so bad," Jimmy said, laughing and shaking his head.

"I always make it up to him later." The elevator doors opened, and they parted ways. Jimmy headed to the geriatrics wing, and Sheila to the pediatrics wing.

He stowed his coat in the usual place and followed a nurse to the room of the new patient.

"Her name is Mrs. Nelson," the nurse explained. "She's very excited about this visit."

"Miss Alicia will not let her down," Jimmy said, stopping in front of the door that the nurse indicated.

He pushed the door open and softly called out, "Miss Alicia the cat is here to visit with Mrs. Nelson. May we come in?" He took a few steps into the room when he saw the elderly woman in the bed. An old man, who Jimmy assumed was Mr. Nelson, stood by her bedside. "Hello, Mrs. Nelson. My name is Jimmy, and this is Miss Alicia."

"Hi, Jimmy," the man said. "I'm Mika, Sylvie's husband."

Jimmy shook Mr. Nelson's hand, undid the zipper on the carrier, and watched as Miss Alicia made her way to the frail-looking woman with clasped hands and tears in her eyes. "What kind of cat do you have at home, if I may ask?"

"Tortie," Mrs. Nelson said in a soft whisper as Miss Alicia settled beside her and licked her hand.

"It's okay. She's just given you permission. Hug away." Jimmy stood back. He never tired of the moments when someone found a bit of comfort in a place known for not much besides sickness and death.

Mrs. Nelson reached for Miss Alicia and picked her up so the cat's paws were on her stomach and the rest of her body was in her lap.

She made nonsense noises while Miss Alicia stared at another worn and withered face that offered nothing but love and affection.

"Well, I'm going to leave you two to be acquainted. If you need anything, or if Miss Alicia overstays her welcome, please let the nurse know, and I'll come and get her right away."

"No way that will happen, Jimmy," Mr. Nelson said, his hand on his wife's shoulder. "In fact you may never get Miss Alicia back."

Jimmy smiled and made his way to the hall, his mind still on Derek. When Jimmy had driven all that way to surprise him, Derek had spent the entire weekend protecting him, opening doors for him, making sure he was happy and content. He'd put Jimmy's every need above his own. Jimmy was sure that Mr. Nelson had done the same for his wife for the past fifty years or so.

Fifty years. He was beginning to imagine what it would be like to devote himself to the same person for fifty years. Fifty years of fun, squabbles, making love, holding hands, sitting and talking as the world around them changed for the better and for the worse. *We won't have fifty years, but, with any luck, we'll have thirty or so.* He arrived at the pediatrics wing.

He was about to push open the doors when he heard his name over the loudspeaker. He was being paged. By whom? Jimmy raced to the bank of elevators. *Oh my God. It's Derek. He's late, but he's finally arrived.*

He tried not to fidget too much while the elevator descended to the lobby. The rides up with Sheila always seemed to be over in a flash. With no one to talk to, the same ride seemed to take forever. Finally the doors opened, and Jimmy turned to face the reception desk. It wasn't Derek. It was Ken.

"Boss," Ken said, reaching for Jimmy's shoulders. "You need to come with me."

"What's wrong? What's happened at the bar? Who's running it right now?"

"Jill is there. The bar's fine. Please, just come with me."

Jimmy nodded and followed Ken outside. When he stopped at a bench, Jimmy was confused, but he waited for Ken to explain. Suddenly, Jimmy thought of Mindy. "Oh my God. Is Mindy okay? Is she here? Is the baby okay?"

"Mindy's fine, Boss. Oh, God, I don't know how to say this." Ken stopped himself, closed his eyes, and took a deep breath. "A police officer called the bar not long after you left. Derek's been in an accident. He's here in this hospital. He's alive, but they're not sure if he'll make it."

Jimmy felt cold all of a sudden. He knew what all of those words meant, knew that there was something wrong with Derek, but he didn't know what to do. And that scratching noise, like someone was trying furiously to get a car to start, was really getting on his nerves. He opened his mouth to ask Ken where the hell that noise was coming from, but Ken had already wrapped his arms around Jimmy's shoulders. "Shhh, I'm so sorry, Jimmy." Ken was saying it over and over.

Finally, Jimmy realized he was making that awful noise.

Chapter 23

JIMMY HAD not been allowed into Derek's hospital room in the ICU, nor would they give him any information. He was not family. So he stood outside, looking through the window, his vision blurred by the tears that fell silently down his cheeks and the only comfort coming from Ken, who had one arm around his shoulders. Jimmy didn't believe at first that the man in all those bandages could possibly be Derek. His Derek was full of life and never allowed anyone or anything to stop him from wringing happiness from every moment. But besides the bits of salt-and-pepper hair poking out from under the bandage and the motionless hands, the person in that bed bore only a passing resemblance to the man Jimmy loved with all his heart.

"Jimmy?" He turned to look at Ken and saw Sheila. She took a few steps toward them and stopped.

"I'm Ken. I work for Jimmy," Ken said, extending his hand.

Sheila nodded and looked at Jimmy. "I'll take Bozo and Miss Alicia home with me tonight. She took his hands in hers. "I know they haven't given you any information, so I spoke with one of the nurses. Derek came through the surgery just fine, honey." She looked around and pointed to a row of seats near a window. The three of them sat, Sheila on one side of Jimmy and Ken on the other, his arm never leaving his boss's shoulder. "That's the good news." Sheila took a deep breath and continued. "Derek sustained a head injury, and they don't know how serious it is yet. They're hopeful that the airbag may have prevented it from being more serious. But, uh, Derek's legs were, uh… damaged. The doctors saved his right leg, but had to amputate the left, just below the knee."

Jimmy felt Ken's grip tighten on his shoulder. "When will they know about the head injury?"

"Once Derek wakes up, they'll have a better idea of what they're dealing with." Sheila patted Jimmy's hand. "In the meantime, Sally is the redhead right over there." Sheila pointed, and Jimmy saw a petite woman bustling around behind the counter. "I've spoken with her and told her that you and Derek are family. She's promised to let you know of any changes in Derek's condition."

"Thank you," Jimmy whispered, wiping at his eyes. "I should go and get my babies and take them home."

"No," Ken said, tightening his grip on Jimmy's shoulders, reminding Jimmy of what Sheila had said a few moments ago. "Sheila has been kind enough to take Bozo and Miss Alicia home with her tonight. And Mindy has the spare bed all set up for you. I'm going to drop you off and then head back to the bar."

Jimmy nodded and stood up. A thought occurred to him as he looked at Derek through the window. "How did the police know to call me?"

"There was a card in Derek's wallet listing you as next of kin," Ken said as he gently guided Jimmy away from the window. "C'mon, Jimmy. Let's get you to bed."

"What if he wakes up and I'm not here?" Jimmy tried to return to the window, but Ken wrapped his arms around his trembling body.

"It's okay, Jimmy," Ken said, stroking his back. "They'll be keeping him under for a few days, I would imagine, from what Sheila says. So, when he wakes up, he needs you strong and healthy. Please, let us take care of you so you can take care of him when he wakes up."

"You and Mindy have enough to worry about," Jimmy said, wiping at his eyes again.

"Nonsense," Ken said. "You helped me when I needed it. Let me do this for you, Boss." Ken smiled.

Jimmy nodded and turned to hug Sheila. "I'll come and get the babies tomorrow? At your house or here?" The three of them started toward the bank of elevators.

"I'll drop them off at Ken's," Sheila said, looking at Ken for permission. When he agreed, she added, "I'll bring them by in the morning. I'll call to arrange a specific time."

"Thank you," Jimmy said. He quickly hugged her again. "Thank you."

"You're welcome, sweetie," Sheila said. She stood back and watched the elevator doors close.

"It's gonna be okay, Jimmy," Ken said as he offered one final hug.

Jimmy wanted to believe him. He couldn't remember wanting anything quite so much.

JIMMY FELT the hand wrap around his waist, and Derek's hair tickled his back. He tried to roll over on his back so he could look at his sleepy smile. This one brief act of tenderness was Derek's way of telling Jimmy that he wanted to make love. It had never mattered whether it was two, four, or eight in the morning. When Jimmy felt Derek's body pressing against his, they gave themselves to each other—as if they'd been doing it for decades.

He tried to roll over, but Derek was whispering softly in his ear. "No, stay right like this. Don't turn around." Jimmy protested, saying he wanted to look at him, see him, feel him, touch him. But Derek was insistent. Jimmy closed his eyes and gave in. He felt the smooth caress along his side and thighs, the strong hands smoothing themselves all over his sensitive skin, and the full lips kissing his neck and ear. He felt Derek's impressive, uncut length moving between his cheeks. He lifted a leg to make Derek's entry easier— but then there was nothing. No hands, no kissing, no Derek.

He rolled over to find no one beside him. There was nothing but a headstone with Derek's name. He reached out to touch it, and the cold stone crumbled to dust at the slightest touch. The dust blew into his face, scratching his cheeks again and again. He tried to call out, but he had no voice.

Jimmy's eyes opened, and confusion overtook him for a brief moment until he noticed Bozo beside him and Miss Alicia surveying both of them from her perch atop his chest.

"Hi, babies," Jimmy cooed softly. The colors in the room and the arrangement of the furniture was off. Something wasn't right. Then he remembered he was at Ken and Mindy's. Everything from yesterday came rushing back to him—Derek lying in the hospital bed, his bandages, his head injury, the loss of his left leg, even Sheila having to find out the information for him since he and Derek were not family.

Jimmy pushed himself up to sit. *He gave my name as the next of kin.* He didn't know why, but that one piece of information brought him a tremendous amount of comfort.

There was a knock on the door.

"Come in," Jimmy said, noticing for the first time that he was in his underwear.

The door opened and Ken popped his head in. "Are you hungry? I can make you some breakfast. Mindy's gone to school already, but I can do pancakes and toast?"

"Ken," Jimmy said as he moved Miss Alicia and got out of bed. "Don't worry about breakfast for me. I'm not hungry. And you and Mindy have been so kind already."

"It's no trouble, Boss, really."

Jimmy put on his pants and shirt, then sat on the edge of the bed to pull on his socks and shoes. "Well, I insist on making you breakfast. Then I need to get Bozo and Miss Alicia home."

"You're welcome to stay as long as you need to," Ken said, shoving his hands in his pockets.

"I know, Ken," Jimmy said, lacing up his sneakers. "And I appreciate it, but I need to be with Derek. Will you be okay to open and close tonight?" Ken nodded, and Jimmy looked around for the carriers. He saw them on a hope chest on the other side of the room. "Will you tell Mindy how grateful I am that you were both there for me?" Jimmy put the carriers on the bed and opened them. Bozo and Miss Alicia walked in willingly.

"We are, you know."

Jimmy saw the earnest look in Ken's eyes and bit his lip. "You know, Ken, I know you think I've been helping *you*, but, uh...." He closed each of the carriers, trying not to embarrass himself in front of his manager.

Ken walked toward him, his arms open. "I know. I know."

Jimmy leaned against Ken. "There was something about you that, I don't know. The more I talked to you, the more I realized you and I were a lot alike." Jimmy wiped at his eyes and took a step back. "Some of us never seem to get any easy breaks, you know? Rough childhoods, too many mistakes to count, shattered self-confidence."

"I know. Mindy saved me from all of that. She never stopped believing, never stopped seeing what you see. I never believed it would ever get better." Ken smiled and put his hands in his pockets again. "You know, I drove by your bar a couple of times and stopped a couple of times, but never went in. Figured I'd get turned down, just like all the other times."

"What made you finally come in?"

Ken shrugged. "Mindy. She would hug me each night after each failure and tell me she was proud of me. So I kept thinking of the day when I could come home and tell her I got a job and kept thinking about the look on her face." Ken sat on the end of the bed. "That's what Derek needs now, Boss. He needs to know that he's got something to work for. He needs to know someone'll be there at the end of that long road ahead."

Jimmy's eyes teared up as he thought of the day when Derek would come home, when the two of them would take whatever heaven would allow. "She's a lucky woman, your Mindy."

"Maybe. But she could have just as easily given up on me." Ken pointed to the carriers. "You can leave them here, you know, until things have settled down a bit."

"I know. Thanks. But I'd like to get them home so they're not too stressed out." Jimmy reached for the two carriers, but Ken was faster. Ken led the way to the car.

"I'll take you to your place, and you can change and get the critters settled. I'll make sure they're fed and taken care of. Mindy told me to tell you she'll come by and play with them, if you want." Jimmy smiled and nodded, glad that Bozo and Miss Alicia knew Mindy and wouldn't be scared or lonely. "Okay, let's get going so I can get you back to the hospital."

Chapter 24

OPEN YOUR eyes. Jimmy stared intently at Derek's battered face. In the eight days since Jimmy had finally been allowed into the room, he'd watched as the colors changed from angry reds to cool blues to bright yellows. The stump below Derek's left knee was no longer wrapped in a thick wad of bandage. The drainage tubes were gone as well. Derek's body was healing. Jimmy's mind had stopped its frantic ramblings or at least had quieted down considerably since that horrible night the week before.

Now he spent most of his days sitting beside Derek's bed, holding his hand, stroking his muscled forearm, willing Derek to open his eyes. He promised him long, luxurious baths and massages to ease his tired body after the physical therapy to come, bribed him with lazy days, just the two of them on the sofa, watching hokey romantic movies. And he promised him nights filled with passion as they got to know each other's bodies all over again.

Nothing worked. Derek was still unconscious. Jimmy had taken calls from Phil and Nick and Clark, each of them as concerned as possible for their longtime friend. Jimmy tried to be upbeat for each of them but started to feel overwhelmed by the questions about when Derek would wake, how long he would need rehabilitation, and whether he would even return to performing. Jimmy had no answers for them. He knew only that Derek was looking at weeks and months of physical therapy, learning to live with a prosthetic leg, and coming to terms with whatever mental and emotional damage the accident may have caused. And that would all be *if* Derek woke up.

Jimmy put his head down and kissed the hands that had held him, caressed him, and pushed the hair out of his eyes.

"I love you, Derek," he whispered against his warm skin. He laid his head down again and stroked his hairy, muscled forearm. He closed his eyes. Without warning, Derek's hand flinched, and the motion carried all the way up his forearm. Jimmy let go and sat back, looking between Derek's hand and bruised face. "Derek?" Jimmy didn't realize he'd been holding his breath until he saw Derek's hand move again, and tears flooded his eyes. "Derek, baby. Open your eyes. It's me, it's your little darlin'."

Jimmy said it over and over, but Derek's eyes did not open. He consoled himself with the idea that it was a first step. He knew that the road ahead would be paved with progress and setbacks. This was a start. And that was good news. He told himself that as he settled his head on Derek's motionless hand. He closed his eyes again, willing another show of progress.

JIMMY WOKE with a start. His head popped off the bed. The room was dark, and he wondered how long he'd been sleeping. He yawned, scratched the back of his head, and noticed that Derek's bed was empty. He jumped to his feet, ready to ask the nurses what they'd done with Derek, but the bathroom door opened, and Derek stood there, covered only in a small towel. He approached Jimmy slowly, his body whole, his face as handsome as ever. He reached out and stroked Jimmy's blond hair. Jimmy opened his mouth to speak but couldn't settle on which question to ask first. Derek put a finger to his lips, his other hand in Jimmy's hair. As Jimmy lost himself in the feel of the man he'd missed so much, his skin tingled, and a cool breeze swept past. He opened his eyes and, once again, Derek had disappeared. The room was stark and empty.

He came awake with a start and raised his head off the bed, weighted down by something tangled in his hair. He raised a hand to free himself, only to realize the weight was Derek's hand. He was awake. Jimmy held Derek's hand and kissed it, not caring that this may be yet another dream. It felt more real than the others. Derek was lying in the hospital bed, his face bruised, his left leg missing below the knee.

Jimmy kissed Derek's hand over and over and lifted himself out of the chair to get closer to his handsome face. "Derek?"

"Dizzy," Derek said, his lips dry and his voice raspy.

"Okay, fine, Dizzy."

"No," Derek said. "I feel dizzy. Hurts."

Jimmy kissed his hand one more time and then placed it carefully back on the bedsheet as he told Derek that he was going to get help. He ran to get a nurse or doctor. They asked him to stay outside so they could check on the patient. He stood plastered to the window, unwilling to move any farther away from his Derek.

He pressed his hands against the cool glass of the window and moved his head when one of the staff blocked his view. *Please, tell me he'll be okay, that we'll be okay.* Jimmy had never asked much from anyone. He'd gone through a lot, lived a lifetime before he even finished high school, and had never blamed anyone or refused to forgive anyone. But as he stood there, seeing Derek awake after what seemed like years, he realized that this wasn't about him anymore. It was about Derek now. Until he was back to his old irascible self, Jimmy would fight as much as he had to.

Jimmy continued to watch through the window. The doctors continued to poke and prod and ask questions. And then Derek's head turned, his eyes focused solely on Jimmy's. The doctors and nurses scribbled things on charts and whispered to each other. Jimmy waited patiently as one of the doctors came out to explain what the next steps would be, that Derek would remain in ICU until he was out of danger, until the specialists could determine the extent of the injuries to Derek's head. After that, if all went well, Derek would be transferred to another wing of the hospital where he would undergo physical therapy.

The doctor was blunt but kind and explained that Derek would be going through a wide variety of emotions over the next few months, or perhaps years. The loss of a leg, the as-yet-unknown damage to his brain, and learning to walk again with a prosthetic were all emotional traumas. Jimmy was trying to take it all in but wanted to grab the doctor by the lapels of his starched white lab coat and yell, "We'll get through all of that. He's alive, and he's awake!"

Finally Jimmy was allowed back in the room. He returned to the chair where he'd spent most of the last eight days, but didn't sit.

"Hi," Jimmy said when he saw Derek smiling up at him.

"Hey, darlin'."

Jimmy laughed and picked up a glass of water and held the straw so Derek could drink. "Don't drink too much. Just tiny sips."

Derek drank while his hand moved to caress Jimmy's thigh. He let the straw go and licked his lips. "They said I've been out for a week?"

"Eight days," Jimmy said, sandwiching Derek's hand between his own. He felt the weak pressure as Derek tried to squeeze.

"What about my leg?"

Jimmy nodded. "Your left, below the knee. They couldn't save it."

"It's gone?" Derek's head came off the pillow, too suddenly, and he winced.

"It's okay. Lie back and rest," Jimmy said, studying Derek's eyes. "Just below the knee. The doctors say you've been very lucky."

"Yeah," Derek said, frowning. "We'll see what they say when they lose a leg and have to use a wheelchair."

"The doctors mentioned prosthetics. They said you'd be a very good candidate because you're in such good shape, and you're strong—"

"I don't wanna talk about it." Derek waved his hand, as if he wanted Jimmy to leave.

"Okay." Jimmy stopped talking, realizing that this was one of those setbacks he'd imagined while Derek was still unconscious. He smiled at Derek.

"Sorry," Derek said, looking sheepish. "Nurse said you been sleepin' here."

Jimmy nodded again. It was another step. Derek didn't wish to talk about it now, shifting the focus to other matters. But Derek would eventually need to talk about everything that had happened to him. Jimmy would make sure he was there beside him. He reached into his pocket, pulled out the key ring, and placed it in Derek's hand. "I want *this* all the time."

Derek looked at the keychain and closed his eyes. As Derek opened his eyes again, Jimmy heard the hiccup and saw the handsome face become contorted. Derek's bottom lip began to quiver. "What am I gonna do now?"

"Whatever you want," Jimmy said, fighting back the tears.

"Finally thought it was my turn to be happy." Derek shook his head and turned away from Jimmy. "How am I supposed to be that now?"

"Do you remember what you said to me when I told you about my scars?" Jimmy didn't wait for an answer. "You told me that I have you to hold on to."

"Not much good to you now, am I?"

"Now you stop that," Jimmy said, using one hand to make Derek face him. "I don't ever wanna hear that again."

"'S true." Tears fell down Derek's face.

"Like hell it is," Jimmy said, wiping his cheeks. "You'll be there for me, and I'll be there for you. Just like I'd always planned."

"Promise?"

Jimmy finished wiping Derek's tears away. "You just try and run me off. You're stuck with me for good now."

"'Kay. I love you, darlin'."

"I love you too."

Derek's eyelids were getting heavier. Probably far too much stimulation for having just woken up to such devastating news.

Jimmy smiled through his tears and watched as Derek closed his eyes. He settled himself back in the uncomfortable chair and felt at peace for the first time in over a week. He suddenly felt exhausted. A week's worth of not knowing, of trying to prepare himself for any of a myriad of possibilities, had kept him going with little sleep and little comfort. But in that brief moment when Derek opened his eyes and recognized him, Jimmy's brain was finally able to turn off.

Before he fell asleep, Jimmy moved the chair even closer to the bed so he could hold Derek's hand. He leaned back one last time and slept.

HE SLOWLY opened his eyes as he became aware of someone stroking his hair. He looked at Derek's bruised face—which held a strange mix of confusion and contentment. He sat up, and Derek's hand fell back onto the bed. Jimmy had been warned that Derek might not always be coherent because of the pain medication.

"Hey, baby. Does it hurt still? Should I call the nurse?" Jimmy stood, stretched his back, and noticed that it was dark outside.

"No," Derek said, seeming a little more coherent. "You need to get some sleep."

"Thought that's what I was doing until someone started messing with my hair," Jimmy said, grinning and reaching for the glass of water. "Thirsty?"

Derek nodded and brought his head up a little, sipping through the straw as he placed his hand over Jimmy's. "Thank you, darlin'."

"God, I've missed hearing that," Jimmy said, placing the glass in one hand and using the other to stroke Derek's hair.

"Don't want you getting sick or... because of me," Derek said, reaching out to touch Jimmy's shirt. "Got plans for us. That is, if you still want a cripple."

"You stop that right now. I'll be fine. We'll be fine," Jimmy said. He leaned over and placed a chaste, lingering kiss on Derek's full lips. "I already told you that I'm not going anywhere. So you just keep making those plans."

"I'm holding you to that promise."

"I'm counting on it," Jimmy whispered in his ear and then stood up again. "Phil, Clark, and Nick were here a couple of days ago. I'll be sure to call them and let them know you'll be back to your old self in no time."

"Hope so," Derek said, his eyes half-closed as he struggled to stay awake. "My kids?"

Jimmy took a deep breath and shook his head. "I'm sorry, baby, but no. It's just been me and your friends."

"Not surprised I guess," Derek said. He reached out to pet Jimmy's shirt again and then moved his hand to rest on Jimmy's hip. "You need to go home, take care of your babies."

"Ken looks in on them," Jimmy said. "So, I'm not going anywhere."

"Stuck with you, huh?" Derek tried to wink. "Good stuff."

Jimmy laughed, not sure if Derek was referring to him or the drugs, and leaned over one more time to kiss those lips and feel Derek's hand move against his belly. Derek wanted to deepen the kiss, so Jimmy obliged him for a few seconds and then pulled away and pointed to the machines whose beeping sounds grew closer and closer together. "Hear that beeping? If it gets any faster, the nurse will come in and throw me out. Now get some sleep. I'll be right here when you wake up."

"I love you, darlin'."

Jimmy stood back and watched Derek's eyes close. He couldn't help but marvel at the serene expression on his face. He would get his Derek back. Perhaps he would be a little bit banged up and missing a part or two, but Jimmy really didn't care. For the first time in over a week, Jimmy's mind raced with thoughts of the two of them in their own little house by the junkyard, making love under the stars, their bodies cooled by the evening breeze. He and Derek would be together and get the chance to live their dream.

He sat back in the chair and looked at the beautiful, damaged body of his man—the only man he'd ever loved—and thought of those moments to come. Jimmy was looking forward to them. Not because they would be together again, but because there would be an unbreakable bond between them. Derek had already proven his devotion to Jimmy. Now it would be Jimmy's turn to prove his.

There would be some long weeks, maybe even months, of rehabilitation—of Derek feeling angry, confused, cheated, and Jimmy offering as much comfort as he could. It might be the toughest test for the two of them, but it wouldn't be the only one. Jimmy was sure of that. But he wasn't about to let this change his mind about spending the rest of his life with Derek. He would be strong enough to see both of them through this, no matter what it took.

Chapter 25

JIMMY LOOKED on as Derek, covered in sweat and cursing like a sailor, threw down the crutch and leaned against the wall. "Why can't I use two? It's easier with two!"

"That's why. Because it's easier with two. You need to learn to walk with one now." Jimmy tried not to laugh as the petite therapist, her hands on her hips, looked up at Derek and met his glare. "You want to use a prosthetic, right?" Derek nodded. "Well, then, you're gonna have to learn to walk with zero crutches. Now, let's try again, and then we'll finish up with some contracture exercises."

"Ah, for fuck's sake, Monique, those hurt too much."

Monique blew a raspberry at him. "Not as much as if you let your muscles atrophy. Don't pretend like you don't know about all this. I've been telling you for weeks now what to expect at each step of this rehab. Even gave all that info to your man. Now let's try again."

Derek looked down at the crutch and then back at Monique. He raised his eyebrows.

"I didn't throw it down there," she said, holding out her arm. "Lean on my arm and bend down and get it yourself."

Derek did as he was told and tried walking again with the single crutch. Jimmy felt enormous relief. He'd never seen this side of Derek, but it was a relief, nonetheless. Especially after Derek was deemed well enough to be moved from the surgery ward to a recovery room. It hadn't taken as long for his wound to heal over and shape as the doctors expected—which was very good news—but Jimmy had not expected Derek to become so lethargic and apathetic toward his rehabilitation.

There were too many days to count when Jimmy would arrive and be met with one- or two-word answers, too many nights when he returned home because Derek did not seem to want to have anything to do with him. But as difficult as it was to endure, as difficult as it was to have Derek refuse to look at him, Jimmy knew that Derek was going through much worse. He had done enough research about amputation, phantom pain, and lost self-esteem. But Jimmy remained optimistic that he would get Derek back. And he did, although this Derek seemed to really like swearing a lot.

"Hi, Derek," Jimmy said as he walked over to the two of them. "Hi, Monique. How are you?"

"Hey, Jimmy. I'm doing great today. And Mr. Roberts here was just telling me how much he misses you." Monique pressed her palm against the back of Derek's residual limb and pressed upward so the knee would straighten.

"Fuck," Derek hissed as he gritted his teeth and held his breath.

"Breathe," Monique cooed. "Relax and breathe." Her free hand massaged and kneaded Derek's hamstring muscles. "Aren't you gonna say hi to Jimmy?"

"Hi," Derek mumbled between breaths, his fists clenching and unclenching with the effort of trying to move his residual limb. "Sorry."

"No problems, darlin'," Jimmy teased.

"Did you want to tell Jimmy the good news?" Monique looked up at Jimmy as she lowered Derek's leg to the mat.

Derek took a deep breath, sat up, and began to massage his stump. "Doctors are discharging me tomorrow."

"And?" Monique was standing beside Jimmy now, a sly smile on her face.

"I'll have another couple weeks of therapy before I can be fitted for a prosthetic. Have to wait for my stump shrinker to stop shaping my stump."

"That's wonderful!" Jimmy kneeled down on the floor beside Derek and gave him a quick kiss on the temple. "That won't be a problem. I can drive him and then pick him up, so whatever time is best for you," Jimmy said to Monique.

"*Him* is in the room," Derek muttered. "And I can drive myself."

"Well, it's nice to see he's even grumpy with you today."

"Not grumpy. I'm tired."

"You say tired, I say pain in the ass," Monique said and held her palm out for Derek. "Good job today, Derek. See you in a couple of days, right?"

Derek high-fived her, reluctantly, and he and Jimmy watched her go. "I'm not a pain in the ass." Derek used his towel to wipe his forehead. "Am I?"

Jimmy laughed and pushed himself up so he was standing. "You may wish to rephrase that question. Especially to me."

Derek looked up at Jimmy, his expression bewildered. Then, understanding what he'd just asked and to whom, he fell back on the mat and laughed. "You're gonna make me buy her a gift basket or something, aren't you?"

"I'm not going to make you do anything, except get up and get in that wheelchair."

"Can I try walking back to my room?"

"You know what will happen if the doctor finds out, right?"

"Please?"

Jimmy looked at the handsome face, flushed from all the recent exertion, and sighed. "Okay, but I'm following you with the wheelchair."

"I'm sorry, darlin'."

Jimmy knew why he was apologizing but was still having fun with him. "What for?"

"You know," Derek started as he sat up again and held out a hand. "I know I haven't been the easiest person to live with lately, but...."

Jimmy held out his arm so that Derek could steady himself as he used the crutch and his good leg to stand up. Jimmy pulled out his keychain and held it up in front of Derek's face. "Did you mean this? The message on this keychain?"

"Yes, of course."

"Then that's all that matters." Jimmy grabbed hold of the wheelchair and walked slightly behind Derek as he steered his way to the exit. "And besides, it's kind of fun watching you get your ass kicked by an eighty-five-pound girl."

"She's one ten if she's an ounce," Derek said, moving closer to the wall for support.

"If it makes you feel better," Jimmy said, a smile on his lips. "Okay, one ten."

Derek's room was on the same floor as the therapy gym, so he didn't have far to go, but Jimmy could tell he was getting tired. He maneuvered the wheelchair and suggested Derek sit. He was amazed when there was no argument.

"So, baby, how was today, on a scale from one to ten?" Jimmy had started asking Derek this question at the end of each day. He started it just after Derek moved to a recovery room and off the surgery floor. It was his way of trying to get Derek to think about the entire day and not just the frustrating or difficult bits. It was something Alicia had taught him all those years ago when they'd been in this hospital together.

"Eight."

Jimmy smiled and turned the last corner to Derek's room. "Maybe tomorrow will be a nine?"

"Can't believe I'm free tomorrow."

"Bozo and Miss Alicia are going to be so excited." Jimmy pushed the wheelchair into the room and stopped beside the bed.

"I've missed them so much," Derek said before hoisting himself out of the chair. He perched on the edge of the bed and held out his arms. "Come here, darlin'."

Jimmy went willingly and stood between Derek's open legs, his hands caressing his head, neck, and shoulders.

"Know what I've missed most of all?"

Jimmy's ears became hot as he thought of how long it had been since he and Derek had made love, since he'd known the exquisite sensation of Derek taking him. He was about to answer, but then Derek was pinching his ass.

"Your cooking."

Jimmy raised his eyebrows and pulled at Derek's chest hair. "Okay. I'm sure we can set a cot up in the kitchen."

Derek laughed and wrapped his arms tighter around Jimmy's waist. His hands felt for the waistband and easily slipped inside. "We need to get some weight back on you."

"And you."

"I think you know what I missed the most," Derek said, leaning in for a kiss. Jimmy obliged him. It was tender but intense. It was a kiss shared between two men who'd almost lost each other—almost had to learn to live without each other again. "I can't wait to make love to you again."

"Go on," Jimmy whispered.

"To see you lying there, naked—your face and chest all flushed—waiting for me to lick and kiss and taste. And when you're panting my name over and over, I'll put your legs on my shoulders and tease your hole before I press inside slowly."

"You should see your face right now," Jimmy said, his breathing growing a little more rapid. He pressed his forehead against Derek's and pushed against his chest with his right hand. "We should stop. Someone might come in."

Derek let go of Jimmy's waist after a few moments and then moved his hands to cradle his face. "I love you, darlin'."

"I love you too, Derek." Jimmy stole a kiss and took Derek's hands. "Monique and the doctors have been very frank with us, telling us what to expect. You know you're going to have good days and bad days, but you also know I want to be there for all of them, for you." Jimmy held up the keychain. "I don't want to miss any of them." Jimmy caressed Derek's cheek. "And if it helps you get through physio, just remember how brave I think you've been, how strong you are." Jimmy raised his eyebrows. "And what I'm gonna do to you when you're finally in our bed again."

"DEREK," JIMMY said. Derek could tell he was losing his patience. "You knew that this could happen. You have to give your body time to adjust."

"Fuck that," Derek grunted through clenched teeth as he rolled off Jimmy. "The one thing that got me through all of this and now look at me. Can't even...." He'd had such plans for their first night together. Jimmy had gone to the trouble of cooking him a wonderful meal. They'd kissed and cuddled on the sofa. And just when Derek thought he could take it further, he'd rushed things and contorted his left leg. The shock had run up all the way to his fevered brain and killed his erection. And no matter how much he concentrated, he couldn't get it back.

"I know it's not easy, but you know it's only temporary. There are plenty of other things we could do."

"I don't want to do other things. I wanted our first night back to be special."

Jimmy cuddled closer to Derek and whispered in his ear. "Do you remember our first night together? In the hotel room? I remember the look on this handsome face. You couldn't wait to get my clothes off, couldn't wait to make me writhe on that bed, scream your name as you kissed me all over and rimmed my ass—the ass you'd been thinking about for so many nights."

"I had to pace myself, you were so fucking hot, Jimmy." Derek looked at Jimmy's flushed face. "I never wanted anyone like I wanted you." He closed his eyes when he felt Jimmy take hold of his cock and massage the foreskin. He was getting hard again.

"You know my favorite part of that first time?" Jimmy straddled Derek's hips, kissed his lips and chin, and licked at his ears. "I'll never forget the look on your face when you pushed all the way in that very first time. Your beautiful eyes looking down at me, the way they fluttered when I squeezed this gorgeous uncut cock. You were amazing, baby. You felt incredible—so big and powerful."

Derek returned Jimmy's fervid kisses as his hands skimmed over his body. He felt Jimmy place his cock at the entrance to his hole. Jimmy sat down, slowly, taking Derek's full length. They stopped kissing only when they needed to breathe.

"You figured out that jacking my cock while you fucked me made me even hotter."

Derek grasped Jimmy's cock and began stroking it.

"I wanted it to last forever. You started out so slowly. In and out, in and out, until I thought my head would explode from the sheer pleasure of being stretched so wide open underneath you."

"God, you were so beautiful. This chest. Those lips. Your hot, tight hole. And the way you touched me, petting my belly and reaching underneath to massage my balls."

"Mmm," Jimmy breathed into Derek's ear. "Like this."

Jimmy massaged his balls, just like he would do each and every time. It meant they couldn't kiss, but it gave Derek time to look at Jimmy's face and chest and focus on stroking his cock.

"And then you called me darlin', over and over while your balls slapped my ass. I closed my eyes and pictured that incredible ass of yours pumping faster and faster while the sweat drenched all that beautiful hair on your pecs."

"Then I found just the right angle and stroked over your prostate, again and again, until you called my name and came in my hand."

Jimmy leaned forward and found just the right angle so Derek's cock would peg his prostate. "Like I'm going to come soon, baby."

"Oh, fuck, yeah, darlin'. Come for me."

Jimmy kissed Derek, and their tongues pushed and slid against each other. He moved his ass, clenching the muscles.

"Come for me, Jimmy. Come on my chest."

"Derek," Jimmy sighed and let go, his seed spilling just where his man wanted it. "Derek," He repeated, over and over, as he continued to contract his sphincter muscles. "Fuck, Derek, what you do to me."

Derek began to thrust in earnest, his desire to reclaim Jimmy his only thought. Jimmy's tongue was in his ear, and that was all it took. He screamed Jimmy's name as he rode out his own powerful orgasm.

Jimmy lay on top of Derek, and they both soothed and petted with their hands. "I kinda like being on top," he teased, kissing Derek's nose.

"Thank you, Jimmy. I didn't mean to be such a pill."

"I know, Derek, I know. But even so, you're my pill. All mine."

Derek used his clean hand to pull Jimmy's face closer. He kissed him several times before smiling into those pretty blue eyes. "Can I make it up to you with a nice long bath?"

"I would be stupid to turn that down," Jimmy said, lifting himself gently off Derek. "It'll give me a chance to work on preventing contracture."

"Great," Derek said, sounding exasperated. "Can't even get away from it at home."

"Quit whining. You've got your very own masseur at home."

"The best kind too. The kind that provides happy endings."

Epilogue

HE OPENED his eyes slowly. The smell of a roasting turkey assaulted him before he realized he was alone in bed. Completely alone. There was no man, no cat, and no dog. This was the first time since he and Jimmy had finished the renovations to their new house that Derek had woken up alone. Before he got up, he called Jimmy's name. Nothing. He called for Bozo and Miss Alicia but didn't hold out much hope. If any of them were home, he wouldn't be alone in the bed.

Derek put his leg on the floor and sat up, wondering why there was no Miss Alicia on his chest and no Bozo cuddled up by his head. A phantom pain registered in his brain, and he reached down to scratch a lower leg that had not been there for almost a year. As he massaged his stump, he wondered why there was no noise at all in the apartment. There were no sounds of cooking, no noise from the bathroom, no noises coming from outside. He pulled on his boxers and his prosthetic leg, walked out to the living room, and called Jimmy's name again.

Where the hell is he? He went to the bathroom to check for a note and found none. There was a wet towel hanging over the curtain rod, so Derek reasoned he couldn't have been gone for too long. *But why take Bozo and Miss Alicia? Today isn't Friday. And they just had their checkups at the vet.*

The uncertainty seemed to attack him from nowhere. Memories of his existence before meeting Jimmy flooded his brain all at once. Losing the leg aside, Derek couldn't remember when he'd been this happy, this content with his life. He'd spent the last year going to prosthetic fittings, continuing his physical therapy, and learning how to deal with the enormous changes that had been thrust upon him. But through it all there had been Jimmy.

He had some rough days when he had felt like giving up, but Jimmy stayed by his side, encouraging him when he needed it and providing a much-needed kick in the ass when he needed that more. Jimmy had not allowed Derek to feel sorry for himself. "We have each other," Jimmy would say when Derek woke up drenched in sweat after yet another nightmare.

Now that Derek was getting better at dealing with the loss of his leg and possibly his career as a singer, he was grateful that he hadn't had to endure these changes all by himself. He ran a hand over his beard as he headed to the kitchen, certain that Jimmy would have left a note somewhere.

He found it on the counter.

> *Be back before noon. Coffee's ready to go, just press button. Breakfast is in microwave, just press start. Love you.*

He smiled and shook his head at how quickly he'd allowed himself to be overcome by the melodrama of finding himself alone. He hit the button on the coffee machine and pressed the start button on the microwave, then headed to the bathroom for a shower and a shave.

Derek stripped off his clothes and removed his leg. Then he got into the shower and let the hot water relax him. He pushed his face under the hot water to soften his beard before picking up the razor and mirror that Jimmy ensured were always there. Derek had told him that shaving in the shower helped his sensitive skin feel less irritated. He wasn't surprised that Jimmy made sure to have the necessary supplies already in the shower by the next morning.

He studied his face as he lathered up his beard. The bruises had eventually given way to scars, and even they were almost faded. There was one across his lower lip, two small inch-long scars near his hairline, and another at a right angle to his left eyebrow. Derek didn't really mind. He was accustomed to his new reflection. Jimmy told him often enough that the scars made him look dangerous and sexy. How could Derek respond with anything other than a smile and a shake of his head? If Jimmy wanted dangerous and sexy, who was Derek to argue? He felt his cock stir at the thought of Jimmy, naked and sweaty, hovering above him, but he did not touch himself. He would wait for Jimmy to return and perhaps talk him into a long love-making session before lunch—maybe out on the deck again.

Of course, just after Derek arrived home from the hospital there had been some frustrating nights, but they'd worked through those difficulties. He had wanted to believe they could pick up where they left off, with Jimmy's body writhing underneath his as he pushed in and out, driving them both to a frenzied climax. But the sensitive skin on his stump had not toughened up enough to allow him to put too much weight on it. Jimmy had found an immediate solution to that problem, as well. And Derek had to admit that listening to Jimmy describe their lovemaking in such detail was more than enough to get both of their motors running.

He ran a hand over his freshly shaved face and washed himself quickly, trying not to lose his balance. He rinsed himself, letting the hot water from the handheld nozzle massage his stump for a few minutes before turning the shower off and reaching for a towel to dry himself. He sat on the edge of the tub and swung his leg over to touch the bath mat and then pushed himself up and hung the towel on the bar beside Jimmy's before putting his prosthetic back on.

Derek returned to the bedroom for a fresh pair of boxers and poured himself some coffee, wondering if he would be alone long enough to continue working on the latest project in his shop—a classic 1953 Chevrolet Corvette. He'd found the chassis in the yard one day and, feeling sorry for himself, made the decision to go back in time and take up the hobby he'd always loved. He leaned against the counter, felt the breeze blow through the house, and closed his eyes. Jimmy had been nothing but encouraging when Derek announced his plans. He even offered to help him.

He laughed as he remembered the day he'd taken Jimmy up on that offer. It hadn't taken too long to realize that his man was a great cook, a wonderful businessman, and an angel sent down to earth to protect everyone who had the good fortune to meet him, but he was completely lost in the garage. Derek would ask for pliers and get a wrench. He would ask for spark plugs and get a pressure gauge. He would ask for a Phillips and get a Robertson. But Jimmy was learning, and Derek couldn't be more proud.

He set the mug on the counter and was about to head back to the bedroom to get dressed, when he heard something crash outside—like a piece of lumber falling and smacking the ground. It sounded as if it were coming from the back of the house. He hurried as fast as he could to the concrete terrace, and then walked slowly, wondering if he should have brought a bat or something. He dismissed the idea. Crime was almost nonexistent in this town.

Nothing seemed out of the ordinary. The barbecue was still there. The tools were still hanging off the side. The patio chairs were still there. The hot tub was undisturbed. Advancing a little more toward the back end of the lot where there were still some old boards lying on the dirt and gravel, Derek saw something move. He took another few steps before he saw something that made him stop in his tracks.

Hiding in the old, decaying lumber was the tiniest, dirtiest little dog that Derek had ever seen. The fur, what there was, was matted and gray. The little ears were caked in dirt and what might have been dried blood, and the huge green eyes were filled with terror.

"Hey, little guy," Derek said, moving awkwardly to one knee. "I won't hurt you. Come here."

The dog didn't move at all, but Derek could see him shaking. He suddenly realized that he was half-naked, wearing nothing but boxer shorts. He didn't want to venture too far off the deck dressed like that and without shoes, so he ran back into the house, covered himself with a robe, and put on a pair of slippers. Before leaving through the kitchen again, he grabbed the containers of leftover hamburgers and sausages that Jimmy had bought him for the previous night's barbecue. He also took a bottle of water.

He was relieved to see the little dog had not moved. He took a seat at the end of the terrace and dumped the sausages in with the hamburgers, freeing up one of the containers. He filled that one with water and slowly pushed it toward the dog, hoping the little guy would trust him enough to come and take some.

"It's okay, little guy. Are you hungry?" Derek tore off bits of hamburger and threw them toward the dog. Some of them landed out of sight, near the dog but hidden by debris. He did the same with one of the sausages. He stopped when he had a half-dozen pieces of meat lying on the ground. He waited and kept talking to the dog.

After what felt like hours, the little guy's hunger won, and he advanced toward the closest chunk of hamburger, hidden behind a messy pile of dirt and lumber. He devoured it, chewing hungrily, his head moving up and down to keep an eye on Derek. Derek smiled to himself and tried not to move. Then the dog started on the next piece of meat. Still Derek did not move.

When the dog came out from the pile of dirt and lumber to nab the more distant prizes, Derek noticed that the little guy was limping. There was something wrong with his rear left leg. Still Derek kept chatting with him, telling him everything would be okay. He thought about how wonderful it would be if he could rescue another puppy who needed a good home.

"You'll have a brother to play with, and a sister. You should hear her purr. The sound will put you to sleep in no time."

The dog, still shaking, was making his way closer to where Derek was sitting. He was cautious. After grabbing each piece of meat he would back up and stare at him. *It's progress.* He threw more pieces of meat near the mutt.

"Come on. Come and eat, you poor little thing." Derek placed several more pieces of meat near the container of water and waited, trying to remain as still as possible. "I'll wear you down. You just watch. You're going to be sleeping in a nice warm bed tonight. I promise."

JIMMY HAD Bozo on his leash and Miss Alicia in the carrier. He'd been promising for a long time that he'd bring them to visit the staff at the shelter that had cared for them so lovingly until Jimmy arrived to make them part of his family. Of course they would also be thrilled to learn of Jimmy's ulterior motive for this particular visit.

"Hi, Pam," Jimmy said to the young receptionist as he walked through the front door. "I finally got around to keeping my promise."

"Hey, Jimmy," Pam said as she stood up and came to stand in front of the counter. "And who are these precious little babies?" Pam got down on her knees and opened the carrier while she cradled Bozo in her left arm. "They're so big and happy. I haven't seen them in what, five months or so?" Bozo was licking Pam's face while Miss Alicia stretched and then started to knead the woman's thighs, preparing for her own type of visit.

"I'm sorry it took so long, but I've been busy."

"I'd imagine you were busy with the move and the renovations, huh?"

"How did you know?" Jimmy's brow furrowed as he looked down at Pam. "I actually just came in to give you the new address."

"Carol."

Just the one word, as if that explained everything.

"Carol's in the back if you want to go see her."

"Thanks. You okay with both of them?"

Pam was giggling as Bozo tried to lick her face. She waved Jimmy to the back of the shelter. He walked through the door that separated the cages from the reception area and immediately wished he could take each animal home with him. It was one of the reasons he didn't visit as often as he should. It was hard to see the animals and not be able to take them all home.

"Jimmy!" A petite brunette put down her clipboard and walked quickly toward him, her arms outstretched. "Finally!"

"I know. I'm sorry about that, Carol," Jimmy said as he closed the distance between them and wrapped his arms around her. "I'm sorry it's taken me so long to visit."

"Nonsense," Carol said, hooking her arm in his and leading him to the back of the vast room of cages. "I was actually going to call you after Thanksgiving."

"Oh?"

"Pam had this great idea about advertising," Carol said as she pointed to the coffee machine. Jimmy shook his head, and Carol continued. "She got the idea while she was surfing the Internet. She thinks it would be a great idea to have a series of pictures of local people with their adopted shelter pets. There would be a caption explaining the special gift or gifts that these shelter animals have brought to their humans' lives."

"Sounds wonderful."

"Your poster would mention that Bozo and Miss Alicia are therapy pets, that they help children and seniors who need special attention." Carol motioned for Jimmy to sit and then perched herself on the edge of the desk. "Or something like that."

"Count me in," Jimmy said as he settled into his chair. "Let me know when and where."

"Great," Carol said, her smile broad and genuine. "And of course you can bring anyone you'd like to the shoot, or to be in the picture, for that matter."

Jimmy cocked his head to one side. "Okay," he said, slowly, wondering if Carol meant anything by the invitation.

"Did you get my e-mail?"

"About Christmas dinner? Yes, I did. Thank you."

"But?"

"I have other plans. But thank you."

"There'll be plenty," Carol said, almost whispering, as she looked over her shoulder. "So if there's someone special you want to bring."

Jimmy laughed and looked down at his shoes. "Okay, what's going on?"

"I may be pushy and known to cross a few boundaries now and then, but I am *not* a gossip. And that's exactly what I told Ken when he told me that you and the new man in your life are shacking up at the old junkyard. I've driven by it on occasion and can't believe what you've done with the place. It looks amazing."

"Thank you," Jimmy said. "Ken?"

"My brother-in-law," Carol said, with a wink. Jimmy chuckled to himself and shook his head. "I'm so happy for you, Jimmy. Ken says he's a really wonderful man."

Jimmy looked up and wondered what he should say to that. During their courtship he and Derek had discovered that they both shared a need for privacy.

"I know I'm overstepping, Jimmy, but I just wanted to tell you I'm happy for you. It's none of my business, and I'll be the first to admit I thought Mindy was nuts for keeping that man, but he's like a completely different person since you gave him that job. And ever since Joey was born." Carol placed her hand over her heart. "The way he is with their son. Amazing."

"Mindy is your—"

"Sister," Carol said, as she stood up. "It's why I sent you an invitation. Mindy told me about you inviting her and Ken and little Joey for a Thanksgiving celebration, so I thought I'd return the favor. Ken and Mindy always have Christmas dinner at my place, with my husband and kids, so...."

Jimmy smiled. "Mind if I discuss it with Derek?"

"Of course not," Carol said, walking back to pick up her clipboard. "And if it's a no for Christmas, maybe you'll come by at New Year's."

"Absolutely," Jimmy said, feeling exposed but not really caring. He'd spent many years hiding his life away from prying eyes. He had always liked his privacy. He had never wanted anything more than to run his own bar and live a quiet, peaceful life. And he'd done just that, not realizing how successful he'd been until Derek entered his life.

"So, let's go and have a visit with Bozo and Miss Alicia," Carol said, taking his arm and turning to leave.

"Uh," Jimmy said, somewhat loudly. "I actually came here for another reason."

"Okay," Carol said.

"Derek has had many dogs in the past, and when he left his—" Jimmy put a hand to his forehead and started again. "I wanted to get a dog for Derek."

"Sounds like my kind of people," Carol said, putting her hands on her hips. "You know what kind he'd want?"

"That's just it. He's had a Saint Bernard, a Chihuahua, and a boxer. So I don't know how to narrow this down." Jimmy remembered something of that day, long ago—something that all of the dogs Derek had rescued had in common. "I know all three of the dogs, well the last two I'm sure of, were all older dogs that he rescued. He doesn't like the idea of older dogs being abandoned."

Carol smiled and turned to her right, walking up the far aisle and then stopping halfway. "Jimmy? Meet Hansel and Gretel. And don't blame me for the names."

Jimmy walked slowly up the aisle, wondering what he would find. While he loved the idea of rescuing any and all animals, Jimmy was always conflicted about the older dogs. There was nothing like the love of an older animal. They seemed to know they were being saved, that they would be loved. And they returned that love tenfold every day. But Jimmy worried about being the one left behind when the animal would finally pass away.

He arrived at the cage and saw the most beautiful dachshunds—two of them. They were approximately the same size and huddled together at the back of the cage.

"Hansel has the blue collar, and Gretel has the pink," Carol said as she opened the cage. "They are brother and sister and are a bonded pair."

"Meaning they can't be separated?"

"We'd prefer they get adopted together, yes." Carol reached into her pocket, took out a treat, and offered it to Hansel, who sniffed it and then took it in his mouth. He went back to his sister's side and put the treat on the towel that was serving as their bed. Jimmy felt the tears starting to form behind his eyes as he watched Hansel nudge the treat toward his sister.

"They're perfect," Jimmy said before he could stop himself.

"Don't you want to know anything about them?"

"No," Jimmy said, staring at the pair. "Unless there's something medical or psychological that I need to know."

"No, nothing like that," Carol said. Jimmy looked over and saw the self-satisfied grin on her face. "I'll get the paperwork started."

"Will it be possible to take them today?"

"I don't think that will be a problem," Carol said as she walked to her desk. "As long as you promise to take them to the vet as soon as possible for a thorough exam."

"I promise," Jimmy whispered, reaching into the cage. He held his hand out so the pair could sniff him. "I promise."

JIMMY CRINGED when he looked at his watch. *I should have called him.* He took Bozo's leash and Miss Alicia's carrier from the garage to the house. He opened the carrier, detached Bozo's leash, and then went back out for the dachshunds.

"Now, I'm going to put you two in the spare bedroom so you can get used to us all. I'll have Derek, your other daddy, come in and say hi soon." Jimmy made his way to the spare bedroom, put the dog carrier down on the floor, opened it slowly, and walked back to close the door. In the event that he was successful in finding a dog for Derek, Jimmy had borrowed some of Bozo's and Miss Alicia's toys and blankets and scattered them throughout the room. Hansel and Gretel could familiarize themselves with their scents and wouldn't be so jumpy when the time came for an official meeting. "Okay, there's food and water over there and newspapers in the closet for now. I'll be coming back, so don't worry." Jimmy would explain to them during his next visit about going outside for training. He looked down at them, huddled together, and smiled at their seemingly relaxed state.

He let himself out of the room and returned to put Bozo's leash and Miss Alicia's cat carrier away. He wondered what names he and Derek would give the dachshunds. They would need to start using them as soon as possible. *Where is Derek, anyway?* Jimmy thought it strange that Derek had not come out to greet him. The door to the workshop was closed, and the bed was made. There was a stray coffee cup on the counter but no Derek.

"Derek?" Jimmy called out as he stood in the middle of the living room. Hearing no response, he looked around for a note. Nothing.

He headed out to the deck to get the tools from the barbecue—they needed a good cleaning—and stopped in his tracks when he saw Derek struggling to hold on to something in his arms. Derek was sitting on the concrete, wearing nothing but boxers and slippers, a wiggling mass wrapped in his robe.

"Shhh," Derek whispered, stroking the gray furry bundle in his arms. "I just got him to trust me. He was hungry and scared, but I lured him over with meat from last night's barbecue."

"Where was he?"

"I heard a noise and came out to investigate, and he was in the back there, hiding behind some of that lumber." Jimmy watched as Derek stroked and cradled the mutt. "That's a good boy. Yes. You're safe now. You're home."

Jimmy approached slowly and sat down beside Derek. "Why are you only in boxers?"

"Wasn't enough time to get dressed. I came out in boxers and then saw this little guy. Went back in to get food for him. I'll tell you later."

"Is there a collar?"

"No. I don't think so."

"We'll have to take him to Carol's."

"I know. I think there's something wrong with his leg."

"We'll make sure we do everything we can for him," Jimmy said as he picked up a piece of hamburger and watched the little dog sniff it and then gently take it. "Were you thinking of keeping him?"

"Absolutely," Derek said and leaned over for a quick kiss. "Is that okay?"

"Of course. This is your house as much as mine." Jimmy leaned over and rested his chin on Derek's shoulder. "One more won't make any difference. We already have one cat and three dogs."

"Did you hear that, little fella? I get to keep you, and you'll have a brother and—wait, what? Three dogs?"

"I got you a surprise," Jimmy said as he reached out to see if the little dog would allow petting. "I'll explain it all later. Have you thought about any names?"

"Funny you should ask," Derek said. "While I was waiting for him to work his way over to me, he kept sniffing around for more food, and ended up losing his balance and falling over a couple of times because of his bad leg." Derek looked at the mutt and then back at Jimmy. "I think I'll call him Dizzy."

When D.W. MARCHWELL is not teaching future generations the wonders of science, he can usually be found hiking, writing, riding horses, trying new recipes, or searching for and lovingly restoring discarded antique furniture. A goofy and incurable romantic, D.W. admits that his stories are inspired by actual events and that he has a soft spot for those where boy not only meets boy but also turns out to be boy's soul mate. After almost fifteen years of working his way across Canada, D.W. has finally found the perfect place to live at the foot of the Canadian Rockies. He still can't believe how lucky he is, and, as his grandmother taught him, counts his blessings every day.

You can contact him at dwmarchwell@hotmail.com.

Don't miss

A Fine Mingling

By D.W. Marchwell

Benjamin "Big Ben" Forrester came from a wealthy family, went to the right schools, and had handsome men falling at his feet. But all Ben has ever wanted is a man to love him unconditionally. Being a firefighter won't bring Ben fame or riches, so where will he find true love and acceptance?

Alistair McInnis lives with his older sister, Abigail, and her deaf son, Jared. Alistair left his job as an editor to take care of his nephew when Abigail divorced and enrolled in law school to provide a better future for Jared. But Abigail is falling in love with the policeman next door, and Jared won't need Alistair forever.

While working with the station house to oversee the rebuilding of a play castle burned down by vandals, Ben meets and falls for Alistair. Can Ben learn what it means to be accepted for who he is? Can Alistair accept that life comes with no guarantees? They soon find happiness is a fine mingling of hanging on and letting go.

http://www.dreamspinnerpress.com

Don't miss

Pictures on Silence

By D.W. Marchwell

When discredited journalist Duncan Spencer is given the assignment to interview world-famous operatic baritone Barkley Reinhardt, he knows it's fluff, but he's earning a living and he hopes it can take him one step closer to recovering his career as an influential and serious journalist. The singer is surprisingly more interesting than Duncan expected, and Duncan decides Barkley, with his reputation of being increasingly difficult and demanding, would make an excellent subject for a biography. When they meet, Duncan is surprised to find that Barkley has become jaded, is dissatisfied with fame and a life of touring, and deeply desires to pursue drastically different passions.

Although they are worlds apart in careers and interests, mutual fear and desperation rushes Duncan and Barkley into romance. But neither man has taken the time to really know the other, believing instead that what one needs, the other can provide. And then, when Barkley finds out that Duncan is planning to write his biography, he assumes Duncan is just like so many others: seeking only to benefit from his fame. How can a romance that started out so wrong-footed survive after such a blow?

http://www.dreamspinnerpress.com

Don't miss

Sins of the Father

By D.W. Marchwell

While volunteering to help prisoners earn their high school equivalency, Charlie Kirby meets Caleb Farmer, who asks his help to write a letter to his long-lost son, Junior, to make amends. Touched by Caleb's story, Charlie agrees to help.

When Charlie manages to track down Junior, he discovers the man has long since changed his name to James Marshall and wants absolutely nothing to do with his father. Charlie understands James's anger; Charlie spent most of his adolescence trying to convince his own incarcerated father to see him, but his father always pushed him away. Now, Charlie has nothing but regret for the past and the lost opportunities, and he wants to spare James the same fate.

But Charlie's attempts to help James forgive and forget become complicated by feelings he hasn't experienced since the death of his husband. For them to have any chance at finding happiness, James will have to end his self-imposed emotional isolation, but will Charlie's efforts bring James closer or push him further away?

http://www.dreamspinnerpress.com

Don't miss

A Still, Small Voice

By D.W. Marchwell

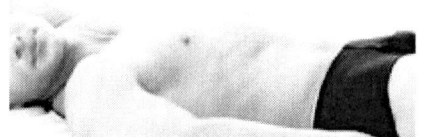

After a student's accusation of sexual assault destroyed his reputation, Noah Lowe left the teaching career he loved. The school system that should have protected him and an ex-lover who should have known better shattered his confidence, and it took Noah six years and another university degree to finally get his life back on track.

He loves his new job as a computer programmer and keeps busy on weekends performing at a drag club with his best friend, Aiden. It's there that he meets shy, chivalrous Oscar, the owner of the club and, just maybe, the love of Noah's life. But everything turns upside down when a specter from his former life moves in next door. Noah will have to face his fears and discover the truth about his ordeal if he wants to move past it once and for all and face the future with Oscar at his side.

http://www.dreamspinnerpress.com

http://www.dreamspinnerpress.com

Good to Know Series

My Best Friend's Brother

CR Guiliano

http://www.dreamspinnerpress.com

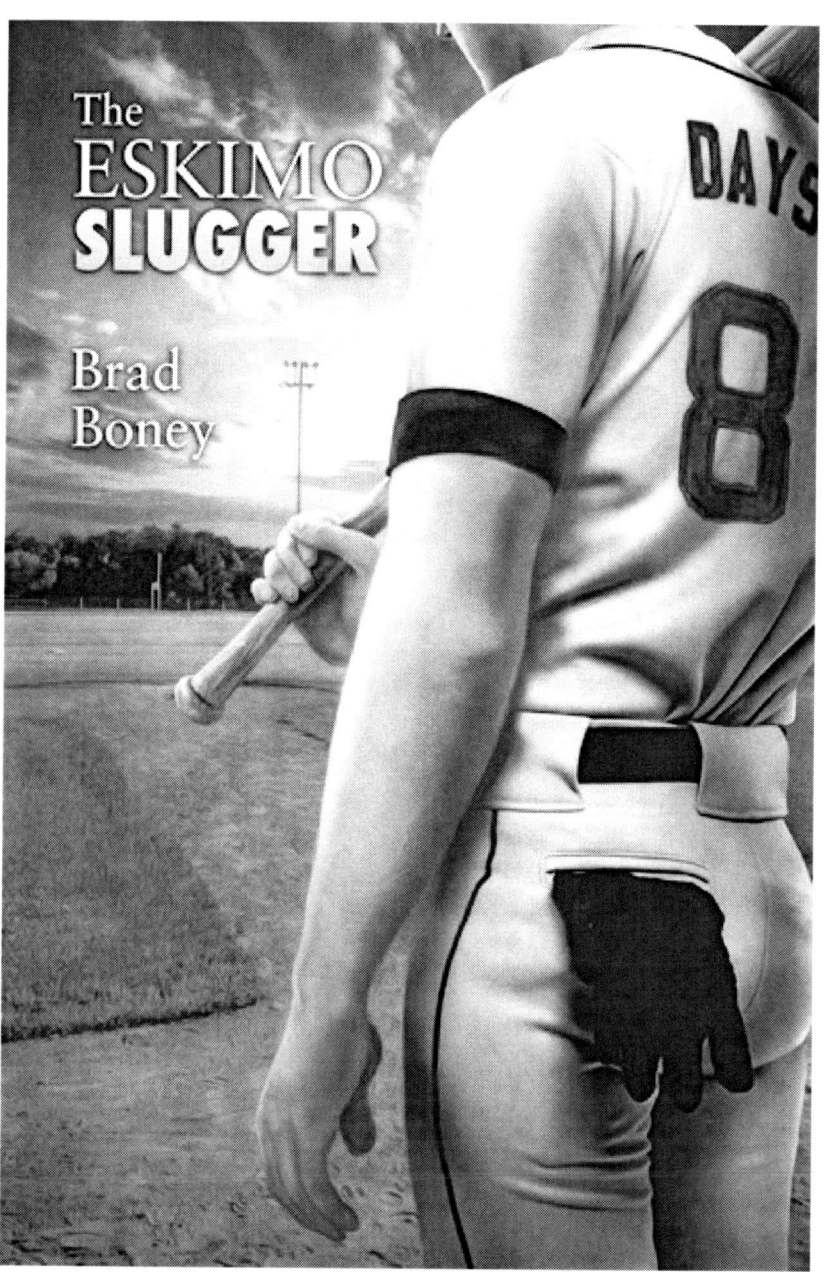

The
ESKIMO
SLUGGER

Brad
Boney

http://www.dreamspinnerpress.com

CPSIA information can be obtained at www.ICGtesting.com
Printed in the USA
BVOW03s1300201214

380037BV00009B/200/P